Nick Blackshe ...... **combination o** ...... **age and single-minded determination.**

He was also far more complex than she'd realized.

"Thank you," she said, then impulsively threw her arms around Nick and hugged him.

She'd meant it only as an expression of gratitude, but the second his arms wrapped around her, she entered a new world—one of fire and longings too strong to resist. As she melted against him, he groaned, and the sound vibrated against her, awakening the woman within.

Nick cupped her face in his hands and lowered his mouth to hers. His kiss was gentle but insistent, coaxing and demanding at the same time. The strength of his arms and the hardness of his body filled her with a sweet, melting heat. The world ceased to exist. There was nothing but him.

At long last he eased his hold. "I'll protect you from others, but who'll protect you from me?"

AIMÉE THURLO

ALPHA WARRIOR

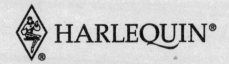

HARLEQUIN®

TORONTO • NEW YORK • LONDON
AMSTERDAM • PARIS • SYDNEY • HAMBURG
STOCKHOLM • ATHENS • TOKYO • MILAN • MADRID
PRAGUE • WARSAW • BUDAPEST • AUCKLAND

If you purchased this book without a cover you should be aware that this book is stolen property. It was reported as "unsold and destroyed" to the publisher, and neither the author nor the publisher has received any payment for this "stripped book."

To Peg. See? You don't have to share!

Recycling programs
for this product may
not exist in your area.

ISBN-13: 978-0-373-69492-1

ALPHA WARRIOR

Copyright © 2010 by Aimée and David Thurlo

All rights reserved. Except for use in any review, the reproduction or utilization of this work in whole or in part in any form by any electronic, mechanical or other means, now known or hereafter invented, including xerography, photocopying and recording, or in any information storage or retrieval system, is forbidden without the written permission of the publisher, Harlequin Enterprises Limited, 225 Duncan Mill Road, Don Mills, Ontario, Canada M3B 3K9.

This is a work of fiction. Names, characters, places and incidents are either the product of the author's imagination or are used fictitiously, and any resemblance to actual persons, living or dead, business establishments, events or locales is entirely coincidental.

This edition published by arrangement with Harlequin Books S.A.

For questions and comments about the quality of this book please contact us at Customer_eCare@Harlequin.ca.

® and TM are trademarks of the publisher. Trademarks indicated with ® are registered in the United States Patent and Trademark Office, the Canadian Trade Marks Office and in other countries.

www.eHarlequin.com

Printed in U.S.A.

ABOUT THE AUTHOR

Aimée Thurlo is a nationally known bestselling author. She's the winner of a Career Achievement Award from *RT Book Reviews*, a New Mexico Book Award in contemporary fiction and a Willa Cather Award in the same category. She's published in twenty countries worldwide.

She also cowrites the bestselling Ella Clah mainstream mystery series praised in the *New York Times Book Review*.

Aimée was born in Havana, Cuba, and lives with her husband of thirty-nine years in Corrales, New Mexico. Her husband, David, was raised on the Navajo Indian Reservation.

Books by Aimée Thurlo

Don't miss any of our special offers. Write to us at the following address for information on our newest releases.

Harlequin Reader Service
U.S.: 3010 Walden Ave., P.O. Box 1325, Buffalo, NY 14269
Canadian: P.O. Box 609, Fort Erie, Ont. L2A 5X3

CAST OF CHARACTERS

Detective Nick Blacksheep—He's an ex-marine with a deadly past and many personal demons. Ordered to drop an important case to protect the niece of the former police chief, he finds his life suddenly turned upside down by feelings that have no place in a warrior's world.

Drew Simmons—She was training for a temporary job in the police records department, but unless she learns to trust her bodyguard, despite all the reasons against it, Drew might become just another crime statistic.

Chief Franklin—He was walking a fine line, trying to protect a friend, but his questionable leadership has already cost him the respect of his department.

Ray Owens—Everyone knows he is the lowest form of human being—a wife beater. But Ray holds a lot of power in the community, and his wrath is now directed at the officer who arrested him—Nick Blacksheep.

Beth Michaels—Once Drew takes over her position at the department, she'll be free to nurse her dying husband—if her money holds out.

Harry Koval—He's responsible for tracking down Drew's assailants, but is making very little progress despite his reputation as a top-notch detective.

Captain Wright—Nick's boss insists on knowing exactly where he and Drew are hiding. Unfortunately, whoever's after Drew is also receiving this information, and that makes Captain Wright a suspect.

Travis Blacksheep—Nick is his older brother, and they've always had each other's back. But someone is now trying to use that against them.

Chapter One

Wherever Nick Blacksheep went, trouble usually followed. That's the way it had been since he'd taken his first breath back on the Navajo rez thirty-three years ago.

Travis, Nick's younger brother, held the punching bag steady as Nick continued to channel his anger into the inert mass. "Work out on this, then we'll go a few rounds," Travis said.

"Wear me down first? Won't work. Right now you couldn't handle me, little brother," Nick growled, and continued to pound the heavy bag.

"Anger destroys focus. I can take you."

"In your dreams," Nick retorted, sinking his taped fists into the thick leather with a lightning-fast combination.

"Have an Enemy Way Sing done. Release the past and the memories of war you still carry inside you and you'll be able to sleep again at night."

"The old ways have no part in my life," Nick said, pounding the body bag with an intense flurry of jabs.

"You need to restore the balance. The path of harmony that allows a man to walk in beauty, the *hózho,* will elude you until you put your ghosts to rest."

"It's the present that's the problem. There's no reason for me to have been put on disciplinary suspension. We've had eight domestic disturbance calls this month alone from that address.

The lowlife there can't keep his fists off his wife. I responded to the last call, and when he tried to slip by me to go whack his wife, I threw him across the hood of his sports car."

"I agree that you did the right thing. But nothing will change until the guy's wife leaves him for good."

Nick slammed his fist into the bag one last time, then stepped back. "I better hit the shower. I've got a meeting with the chief and the review board tonight."

"Everyone in the department knows you're a good cop, and there's enough evidence to clear you. Providing you don't screw up tonight, you'll be fine," Travis said. "Things have hit bottom so they have nowhere to go but up."

"I have my own saying. Just when you think it's really bad, it gets worse."

"Your main problem, bro, is that you substitute attitude for patience."

"I'd rather push things to get them rolling than play nice," Nick said, removing the tape from his knuckles.

Travis shook his head. "A little patience gets better results. Remember how it was for us."

Nick met his brother's eyes. They'd been watching each other's backs since the day their father told them he was going for a walk in the desert and never returned. To this day, they never figured out if he'd meant to abandon them, or had been trying to do them a favor. On the rez, when a man knew that he was dying, he'd sometimes walk off like that. That last act was considered a gift to his family, since a death in the house meant that the building would have to be abandoned. The Navajo Way taught that the *chindi,* the evil in a man, would never be able to merge with Universal Harmony, so it remained behind, posing a threat to the living.

"I'll let you know how things go," Nick said.

WHEN NICK STEPPED INTO the shower, he could hear Travis punching the heavy bag. Travis had lightning-fast reflexes.

Nick lacked his brother's speed and agility, but he packed more power and could slug it out toe-to-toe with anyone.

Fifteen minutes later, Nick was dressed and ready to leave. Tugging on his boots, he stood and automatically reached for the detective's badge he normally kept on the dresser. The empty gesture made him curse. Suspension meant no department firearm *or* badge.

As Nick walked down the hall he saw his brother still working out in the gym they built. They'd worked hard to make what had once been a "fixer-upper" in the middle of nowhere into the perfect home for two bachelors. Marriage wasn't in the cards for either of them. They'd already seen too much of life to settle down with a wife and become a role model for rug rats.

THE RIDE INTO TOWN was open road, most of it down a river valley flanked by wide mesas. Nick pressed on the accelerator and felt the Jeep respond. He liked speed and the edge of danger it brought.

Before long, he entered a west side, high-end housing development, complete with a six-foot wall opposite a private golf course.

His thoughts were focused on tonight's meeting when he came upon an apparent TA, a traffic accident, just ahead in the right-hand lane. Two vehicles, an old sedan and a big van, were side by side, contact point at the front end, just off the road. Their headlights and taillights were still on. Closing in, he noted the fresh grooves on the driver's side of the sedan. From the looks of it, it appeared that the van had cut off the sedan and made contact—not that uncommon. At least neither vehicle had rolled or had plowed into the fence.

Nick stopped, and as he switched on his driver's-side spotlight, he heard a blood-curdling scream. Two large figures wearing hoods were gripping a woman by the arms, trying to drag her around the rear of the sedan.

Fighting like a wildcat, she suddenly broke free. She slammed her clenched fist into the face of the man on her right, swung and kicked his partner in the groin, then raced along the fence line toward Nick.

Giving her room to pass by on his right, Nick pressed down on the accelerator. Intent on scattering her assailants, he drove right at them, giving them two choices—jump out of the way or become a hood ornament.

Chapter Two

Drew Simmons raced down the roadside drainage ditch. The man in the Jeep who'd gone after the ones chasing her had probably just saved her life, but there was no time to thank him.

Tires squealed behind her, but she didn't dare look back. The men chasing her were armed, and the greater the distance between them, the more difficult the shot. Drew struggled to reach the cell phone in her jacket pocket, but it had slipped down beneath where she'd stowed her glove.

As the sound of the vehicle approaching from behind grew louder, Drew swerved to her left, out of the ditch, and leaped onto the fence, grabbing the wire as high up as she could.

The black Jeep came to a screeching stop beside the curb, the acrid scent of burning rubber filling the air.

"Get in," the man yelled. He threw open the passenger's side door. "Hurry."

She dropped to the ground and climbed in. The man she'd kicked was now sprinting down the road, heading straight for them, waving a pistol. The other was in the van, whipping around in the street, tires screaming. They'd catch up in seconds.

"One of them has a gun," she said.

"Fasten your seat belt and hang on," her rescuer said.

He pressed down on the accelerator, and she was thrown

back against the seat. Drew felt around for the seat belt, snapping the shoulder strap in place. A determined look settled on her benefactor's hard features. There was something vaguely familiar about the Navajo man, but she didn't have time to give it much thought.

"There's a shotgun on the rack behind us. The number for the safety lock is two-six-zero-zero. Get it loose before they catch up," he ordered.

Having been raised around guns and taught about safety, she was familiar with the lock and storage rack. Within a few seconds she'd freed the long weapon, swung the barrel up around in front of her, and pumped a round into the chamber.

He looked at her, surprised but happy with her knowledge of guns. "Cool under pressure. And you can fight. That's probably what saved you."

"I know where to kick."

"That's good enough."

The van had stopped to pick up the running man, but was now closing in on them.

"The police station isn't far. Head there," she said, looking back in the side mirror and seeing the dark van less than two car lengths behind.

"If I do, they'll figure out what we're doing and take off. We need another plan. There's no time to call for backup, either."

"You sound like a cop."

"Detective Nick Blacksheep at your service," he said.

"I'm Drew Simmons," she answered. "I'm not an officer, but we work at the same place. So how do we sucker them in?"

"I like the way you think, Drew Simmons," Nick said, and grinned. "Hang on. I'm going to pull into the golf course entrance. It's a dead end. Once I stop, jump out on your side and use the Jeep for cover. I'll take the shotgun. If they start shooting, make sure you stay behind the engine block."

Nick pulled into the dead-end street. Quickly swerving to his left, he took the Jeep into a slow skid, stopping sideways to the street entrance.

Nick took aim with the shotgun, bracing it across the hood. "Stay down," he yelled.

The van's brakes squealed as the driver skidded to a stop, the lights illuminating the Jeep.

"Police officer. Out of the van, hands where I can see them," Nick yelled, averting his eyes to avoid looking directly into the lights.

The van's engine roared as the driver slammed the vehicle into Reverse, burning rubber.

Nick stepped out from behind the Jeep, and squeezed off a round of number four buckshot at the van's driver-side front tire. Sparks flew from the ground as the vehicle fish-tailed violently.

"Stop! Police!" He fired and struck the front of the van just above the bumper.

The van continued in Reverse, then the driver hit the brakes hard. The van whipped around a full hundred and eighty degrees and raced away from them.

Nick switched the shotgun to his left hand and reached into his pocket for his cell phone. "I think I holed their radiator. They won't get far—I hope," he said, watching the taillights disappear into the darkness.

Drew heard him calling in his report as she joined him. "Why weren't you carrying your service handgun? Because you're off duty?" she asked. "No, never mind. I remember now. You're the Blacksheep brother who tossed Ray Owens over the hood of his car. Speaking for most of the women in the PD, we stand ready to buy you the best dinner in town."

"You said you worked for the PD, but I don't think I've seen you before," Nick said, his gaze taking her in slowly and very thoroughly.

She suppressed the shiver that ran up her spine. He was every bit as good-looking as everyone had said, but it was that intense look he was giving her, as if he could see directly into her soul, that made her tingle all the way down to her toes. "I was supposed to take over as head librarian here in town, but the hiring freeze has me doing temp work for city government instead. Right now I'm training to take over for Beth Michaels, the department's record clerk."

"The library's loss is our department's gain," he said, giving her a steamy smile.

Her brain suddenly went into neutral and she didn't know what to say. Horrified by her own reaction, she cleared her throat and tried to appear calm and collected. "Thanks for helping me out," Drew said. "I'm glad I met you, Detective Blacksheep." Drew extended her hand, then quickly pulled it back. "I'm sorry. I just remembered that people from your tribe don't like to shake hands."

"Not with an enemy, or a stranger, but you and I are now connected," Nick told her.

His hand felt calloused and hard as it enveloped hers. Everything about him looked tough and unyielding—and incredibly and irresistibly male. No wonder half the women in the department had fantasies about him. Nick and Travis Blacksheep were the hot, number-one topic on the clerical staff's minds.

As Nick answered a call and walked away for privacy, she gazed at him. He was wearing a brown leather jacket, so she couldn't see much about his upper body, except for his wide shoulders. The dark slacks he wore fit him closely and revealed the best buns in the county.

Drew sighed and tried to remember everything she'd heard about Nick Blacksheep. Word had it that getting him interested in anything more than a one-night stand was like trying to capture the wind. The only person he was close to was his brother, Travis.

Nick slipped the phone back into his jacket pocket and joined her once more. "Why were those men after you?"

"I have no idea. By the time I noticed the van, it was too late to do anything but react. They sideswiped my car, forcing me into the ditch. I got out of the car and ran, but I didn't get far. They were dragging me back to their van when you came up. The rest you saw." Drew swallowed hard. She'd come through it alive and unhurt, and that was the important thing. "It's over," she said, for her own benefit.

"I know you don't want to think about what happened anymore, but I need to you stay focused and remember as many of the details as you can," he said.

He was right. She took an unsteady breath. "For a minute or two I wasn't sure what was going to happen to me. Then..." Her voice suddenly broke and she forced herself to swallow, determined not to cry. She wouldn't fall apart, not now.

Nick came closer to her, almost touching, yet not. "You're all right now, Drew. No one's going to hurt you."

He stood just inches away, and for one brief moment she became aware of everything about him. His scent was earthy and male, and called to her wordlessly, sparking her imagination and teasing her senses.

"You handled yourself well and showed a lot of courage tonight," he said, his voice soothing, even as danger gleamed in his eyes.

"Fear gives you the ability to do things you never dreamed possible," she said.

He nodded, understanding. "Yes, it does." He glanced over at the ditch bank. "Now let's go back to your car and check out the damage."

THEY WERE BACK AT THE original scene a few minutes later and Nick parked about fifty feet away from the rear of her sedan. The right front tire, resting at the bottom of the shallow drainage ditch, was stuck in soft ground. The dome light was still on, and her passenger-side door was ajar.

They climbed out to look, standing in the dim glow of the streetlight. When it appeared that she intended on moving closer, he grabbed her arm. "Better stay on the pavement. We have to preserve evidence, like those shoe prints in the soft sand. This wasn't an ordinary carjacking."

"What makes you say that?"

"Your car…isn't new," he said after a beat. "There's no market for it, intact or stripped for parts."

She gave him a weak smile. "Translation—it was a rolling wreck even before I got forced into the ditch."

As a chill wind whipped past her, she shuddered. "My coat's on the ground near the passenger side. I slipped out of it when they first tried to grab me. Can I go get it if I watch where I step?"

"Better not. That's evidence. If they handled it there's no telling what they left behind for the lab techs," he said, then took off his leather jacket and placed it over her shoulders.

"Now you'll be cold," she said, feeling the warmth of his jacket envelope her.

"I'm wearing a wool sweater. I'm fine."

Sirens rose in the distance, and soon two police units pulled up, emergency lights flashing. A patrolman emerged from the nearest cruiser, and a second later a plainclothes officer with a badge clipped to his belt came out of the unmarked vehicle.

Recognizing Detective Harry Koval, Nick tried not to scowl. Koval and he had a history—and it wasn't a good one. They'd worked as partners for about six months, right after Nick made detective, but Koval's strictly by-the-book, compulsive methods had nearly driven Nick out of his mind. Police work wasn't an exact science, yet Koval did everything lockstep without even a trace of insight or initiative.

"I'm Detective Koval," Harry told Drew, then gave Nick a

cold stare. "You were here when it went down, Detective, so fill me in."

Nick stepped aside with Koval and gave him the highlights. "The only other thing I can tell you is obvious. Considering the wreck she was driving, it definitely wasn't a carjacking."

"Probably not," Koval conceded, looking at the car. "She's young and attractive, and that makes her a different kind of target. Predators are always out there. So what do you think—attempted abduction?"

"Could be. But the fact that there were two perps doesn't fit the most common profile. Rapists usually act alone."

As Nick watched her, he saw Drew cross her arms and press them tightly around herself, seeking warmth, or maybe comfort. Her vulnerability tugged at him and he felt a sudden surge of protectiveness he hadn't expected.

"You still with me, Blacksheep?"

Nick focused, nodding. "Let's go talk to the victim."

Koval spoke first, and, after announcing that he would be investigating the incident, got right down to it. "Describe the men who came after you."

"They were a little shorter than you are," Drew said. "The taller was maybe five-ten, the other a few inches shorter than that. They had on dark jeans and dark blue or black sweatshirts with hoods they'd pulled over their heads. I couldn't see their faces. It was too dark," she said. "That's part of what made things even scarier," she added, in a whisper-thin voice.

"But the extra adrenalin gave you the edge you needed," Nick said.

Koval glared at him, then continued. "Would you say the men were on the thin side, or maybe the opposite, a little chunky?"

She considered it before answering. "They weren't overweight, or overly skinny either. Just average, I guess."

"Any idea why they targeted you?" Koval pressed.

She shook her head. "It must have been random. I never

noticed anyone following me, and I don't have any enemies," she said, despite the skepticism on Koval's face.

FOR THE NEXT TEN MINUTES, Drew gave them her version of the kidnapping attempt, and it coincided almost perfectly with what Nick had reported.

"Has anyone shown any special interest in you lately— maybe at work, or at the grocery store or in your neighborhood?" Koval asked. "Anywhere?"

Nick saw her struggle with all the raw emotions that were crashing around inside her head, and wished he could do more to help. Then he saw the flicker that swept over her features, and he knew Koval had been right to press her.

"Something odd did happen to me a few days ago. I was at the Westside Mall and a man kept following me. He didn't try to talk to me or anything, but it got a little creepy. After a while I went to find a security guard, but when I went to point out the guy, he was gone. I figured that it had probably been some poor guy shopping with his wife and he'd just happened to be wandering in my direction. I'm not the only woman who shops for special shoes."

Thinking she meant orthopedic wear, or something of that nature, Nick automatically glanced down. As he saw what she was wearing, he bit back a smile. They wouldn't go under a handicap header—but, dang, it took guts to wear those. Her sneakers had bright pink polka dots and glow-in-the-dark shoelaces.

"What did the mall guy look like?" Harry asked, his focus strictly on business.

"He was around five foot seven, or maybe eight, brown hair cut short. But that's all I remember. I never looked directly at the guy because I didn't want to encourage him."

"But you haven't seen the subject since?" Koval said, bringing her back on track.

"No. I lead a quiet life, Detective. My uncle's the former

chief of police, Earl Simmons," she said. "The troublemakers in town know that, too, and generally avoid me."

"Until now," Koval said.

Nick hadn't made the family connection until that moment, but that explained a few things, like her skill in removing the safety lock on a weapon and her ease in feeding a shell into the chamber of his short-barreled shotgun.

"Lately, I've been working very long hours," Drew said.

Koval nodded. "I know. Right now, you're training to take over for our records clerk, who's about to go on an extended leave of absence. You and Beth know each other, so I imagine that gave you the inside track."

"No, sir," she snapped. "I got the job on my own merit. In addition to my degree, I have three IT courses under my belt. I was the most qualified person available."

Koval gave her one of his famous stares. They'd been known to intimidate all but the most hardened of criminals, but Drew met his gaze with an unflinching one of her own, and held it.

Nick had trouble biting back a grin. He liked this woman more with each passing second.

"I want you to come down to the station and look through our photo arrays. See if anyone there looks like your mall stalker," Koval said.

"Right now?" she asked, then pointed to her damaged car.

"Perhaps Detective Blacksheep can give you a ride," Koval said, and glanced at Nick, who nodded.

"Before I go, I'd like to get my purse. It's still on the front seat," Drew said. "No one touched it, or even got near it, except me."

"Your sedan's part of the crime scene, so it'll be towed in as evidence. But one of our officers can retrieve your handbag for you," Koval said.

They waited as Koval spoke to a member of the crime scene

team. The tech then walked over to her car and brought out her big tote. The stubby, barrel-chested man carried her purse like a grocery bag instead of by the handles, and handed it to her without comment.

"Thank you," Drew said.

The man nodded, obviously glad to have it out of his hands.

Drew walked with Nick back to his Jeep. She'd never been the kind to be overly affected by a guy's looks, yet there was something about Nick that made her a little crazy inside. Maybe it was that cold, hard gaze that softened, and even warmed, when he looked at her, or that rugged masculinity that assured her she was safe by his side.

She shook her head, trying to unscramble her thinking. She was confusing feelings of relief and gratitude with… something else. Or maybe she was simply trying to distract herself from the horrible incident she'd lived through. She'd never been impressed by macho men, and after a lifetime of living with cops, she definitely didn't date them.

Stopping by the outer edge of the yellow crime-scene tape strung around the perimeter, Drew glanced back at her car. "Do you think anyone would mind if I also took the book bag in the backseat? The two who came after me never touched that either."

"What's so important about those books?" he asked.

"They're reference manuals that belong to the police department, and I don't want to leave them in the impound lot. Without those, I can't complete my training."

"Let me consult the crime-scene team leader." Moments later, Nick returned holding a heavy nylon backpack and handed it to her. "Here you go."

"Thanks." She slung the straps over her shoulder and once again fell into step beside him.

They soon reached his Jeep and got on the road. Out of the corner of his eye he saw her shudder. "Are you okay?"

"No, I'm not. I'm scared. I still don't know if I was a target of opportunity or their intended victim. I also don't know when—or if—they'll come back and try again," she said, her voice rising an octave.

"You really don't have anything to worry about. Your uncle has a lot of clout with our department, and I'm pretty sure that he'll insist the new chief provide you with protection until we know more about what happened tonight. The fact that you're Earl Simmons's niece puts an entirely new spin on things. What happened to you tonight may be linked to him and something he did as a police officer years ago. Revenge can simmer for a long time."

"But logically, if they wanted to get at my uncle, wouldn't they have gone after my aunt instead of me?"

"Maybe you were more available. Or it could have all been just a matter of timing."

Drew considered it, then shook her head. "Your answer doesn't feel right to me."

"It doesn't—what?"

"Call it intuition if you want, but I trust my instincts. They've always been reliable."

He wasn't a big believer in instincts—a woman's or a man's—but sometimes what people attributed to instinct was nothing more than the product of subconscious observations. "So what do those vibes tell you now?"

"That my troubles are just beginning," she whispered.

"Evil is never easy to face down, but you're doing just fine. Those men are nursing some bad bruises by now. Not bad for a librarian," he said, with an easy smile.

Chapter Three

While Drew looked through the mug shots, Nick reported to Chief Franklin's office. Captain Wright, Nick's immediate supervisor, was already there.

"I got an earful from Earl Simmons," Chief Franklin said, muttering an oath. "He still monitors police calls and knew what went down minutes after it happened. He doesn't seem to get the fact that he's not police chief anymore. If that bullet hadn't put him on the disabled list, there's no way that man would have retired."

"What can you tell us about tonight's incident, Nick?" Wright asked.

Nick gave them the facts, then added a couple of his own theories regarding possible motives. "Koval's just getting started with the investigation, but he's like a pit bull when it comes to cracking a case. He won't back off until he's got the answers he needs."

"All right then, let's get back to the original reason you were coming in tonight—your hearing," Chief Franklin said. "The rep from the officer's association is waiting for us in the conference room, and so's the civilian lodging the complaint— Ray Owens. He's threatening to sue the department and you personally."

"I stand behind my actions. They were entirely within department guidelines. I've done nothing wrong," Nick said.

"All right. Let's get to it then." Chief Franklin led the way out of his office and down the hall.

When Captain Wright paused at one of the rooms to speak to another officer on duty, Nick slowed his pace. He didn't want to go into the conference room until everyone was there.

As he waited, Owens came up, blocking his way.

"Say goodbye to your career, hotshot. By the time I'm through with you, you'll be lucky to get a job mopping the restrooms," he said, his voice loud enough for only Nick to hear.

"Get out of my face," Nick growled.

"And if I don't, then what? You'll take a swing? Go ahead. We've got a roomful of witnesses," he said, jabbing Nick in the chest with his fingertip.

Nick grabbed Owens's index finger and bent it back enough for the man's eyes to water.

Owens staggered back, bumping into the doorjamb, and looked around quickly for a witness, but it was fruitless. Everyone was pretending to be looking elsewhere—except for a man in an expensive business suit. Nick guessed he was the wife beater's attorney. His word wouldn't carry very far in this gathering.

Drew, who'd come down the hall along with her uncle, stood back as former chief Earl Simmons stepped up. Giving Owens a look of pure contempt, he glanced over at Nick. "I caught all that, if you need a witness, Detective Blacksheep."

Owens glared at Earl.

"Let's just get this over with, Ray," Della Owens said, interrupting the face-off by taking her husband's arm and leading him into the conference room.

Nick glanced back at Drew before going into the room. She smiled and gave him an encouraging thumbs-up, signaling him that she'd also seen enough to know the truth.

DREW TOOK A SEAT IN THE staff office, her uncle Earl on one side, Beth Michaels on the other. Beth had been at the station when she'd heard about the attempted kidnaping, and had decided to stay, knowing Drew would be coming in. Beth had custody of the photo arrays—the mug files—mostly computer images these days.

"Ray Owens is an idiot," Beth said. "Even if Della refuses to defend herself, as an officer of the law, Nick had to step in."

"So what happens now?" Drew asked, watching the officer on duty confronting the reporters in the front lobby.

"Chief Franklin will do what's right for the department, but Owens has a lot of pull in this town, and the best friends money can buy. He and I have had our own run-ins. I still say the reason he beat my firm out of a construction contract with the state was because he had inside information."

Earl looked directly at his niece. "Right now, you've got other, more immediate problems. You have to move back in with Minnie and me until we know it's safe for you to be on your own."

"I appreciate what you're trying to do, but I can't bring that danger home to you and Aunt Minnie."

"I can protect you both," Earl said, his expression hard, his voice flat.

Though he wasn't the department's chief anymore, that take-charge attitude still clung to him. Giving orders came as naturally to him as it had to her dad. She thought back to the days when her father had been alive. She'd always followed his orders. He wouldn't have had it any other way. Then, after her parents' death, she'd gone to live with her uncle, who'd also ruled his home imperiously and absolutely. But she was an adult now, and would decide which course was right for her. Uncle Earl missed police work and wanted to be part of the fight, but she wouldn't expose her aunt to the dangers she was facing.

Other officers soon came into the common area, often labeled the bullpen, and Drew's uncle walked away to talk to old friends.

Hearing loud voices coming from the conference room, Beth glanced over at the closed door. "I will never understand why Della puts up with that creep."

"All Nick did was defend the victim of an abusive husband. How did that ever get turned into a charge of police harassment?" Drew asked.

"Della changed her story. She's now saying that she fell down. Without her testimony, and no witnesses to what actually happened, at least inside their residence, Nick's the fall guy."

"Owens is purposely trying to put the department on the defensive, hoping to distort the truth," Drew said.

"Exactly. Since that's the umpteenth call our officers have answered at Owens's house, Ray's only way out these days is to claim police harassment. But everyone knows the truth, so the only option Owens really has is to cut a deal of some kind."

The door to the conference room opened and Nick came out alone.

Earl Simmons went to meet Nick just as Owens and his wife came out. With Ray in the lead, the pair hurried toward the exit. Della's head remained down and she avoided eye contact with anyone.

Chief Franklin stepped out of the room next, and joined Nick. "You're reinstated, Detective Blacksheep," he said. "Pick up your service weapon and badge from the duty officer and get the MDT back in your vehicle," he said, meaning the mobile dispatch terminal computer officers carried.

"How's this really going down on paper?" Nick asked the chief.

"Mr. Owens will probably never admit spousal abuse, but he's dropped his charges against you and the department and has agreed to enter anger management and couples counseling. It's a win all around," he said.

"I'm glad that you convinced your old friend to see reason," Earl said to Franklin. Though he'd deliberately kept his tone casual, the point had been made. "But you've still got another problem—me. My niece needs police protection."

Chief Franklin crossed his arms across his chest. "You're assuming they'll go after her again, Earl, and there's no proof of that. I'm not sure I can spare any of my officers on speculation alone."

"You didn't have a manpower problem when you put your best detective on suspension," Earl said, cocking his head toward Nick. "That suggests you can spare him again."

Chief Franklin glanced toward the office area, catching Koval's attention. "What's your take, Harry?"

"Some protection seems appropriate," Koval said. "The way things went down indicates a certain level of planning."

Drew glanced around the room. She wouldn't have minded some extra patrols around her apartment, and maybe someone who'd drop by—often—but she didn't like being discussed as if her right to decide for herself had suddenly vanished. That's the way it had been most of her life, but she was on her own now and didn't have to take orders from anyone.

She was about to make her wishes known in no uncertain terms, when Captain Wright suddenly whispered something in the chief's ear.

A moment later the chief looked up at her, then at Nick. "Detective Blacksheep, you've had more than your share of publicity lately. Photos were taken of you tonight by those reporters outside the building, and they're probably already on the Internet and will be in the local paper by morning. Since you've become a high-profile officer, your undercover assignments are effectively over, so I'm assigning you to protect Drew Simmons until further notice. You'll report to Detective Koval and Captain Wright. They'll update me."

"Chief, you can't pull me off my cases," Nick protested. "I'm getting close to identifying Coyote. I've got a photo to work with now, so it's just a matter of time before I can get his real name, and maybe set up a sting. Let me see this one through, otherwise months of work will be lost."

"You have your orders. Turn over your active case files, photos and all, to Detective Koval. He'll reassign them to other detectives."

"Wait one darned minute," Drew said, finally managing to get a word in. "I have a say in this, too, and there's no way I'm going into protective custody and hiding out. I'm in the middle of training for a job with this department and I need to finish what I've started. I support myself, and that means I need to work."

Earl narrowed his eyes at her, then in a voice that left no doubt he was issuing a direct order, told her, "Take the protection, Drew."

"Your job will be held for you," Chief Franklin added, and looked at Beth, who nodded.

"Keep the reference materials and your laptop, and you can study away from the office," Beth said.

"For the time being, I see no reason why you can't come to work, too," Chief Franklin added. "There's no safer place for you than this station. Detective Blacksheep can work out the particulars for you."

"Ms. Simmons will need a place to stay starting tonight," Nick said.

"Accompany her to her residence so she can pick up some essentials, then take her to one of our safe houses," Franklin said.

Drew fought hard to stay calm. She didn't want to be placed in anyone's care. Yet, to turn down police protection would mean risking another encounter with the men who'd come after her.

She took a deep breath. If she had to accept help, then

it would be on her own terms. She'd take responsibility for herself and demand a say in every decision that affected her. Not that Nick would make that easy. He was obviously strong-willed—but so was she.

NICK LED DREW ACROSS the bullpen and picked up his badge and handgun from Captain Wright.

Nick then went to his bullpen work station and began transferring his case files to Koval's network folder. "I could have closed this gun-running case if I'd been given just a little more time," he said, and muttered an oath.

"This is no picnic for either of us," Drew answered, putting on a borrowed coat. "But maybe this will be over soon. Detective Koval might find some answers after he does a little more digging." Seeing the open skepticism on Nick's face, she added, "But you don't think so, do you?"

"Unless it's an ex-boyfriend stalker, cases like these can often take weeks—or months," he said, then finished transferring the electronic files to Koval. Taking folders containing the hard copies from his bottom drawer, he strode over to Koval's desk and dropped them down with a thump. "My files and my notes. Now you've got everything."

"You said you were close to identifying the arms dealer supplying those cartels south of the border. Just how close are you?" Koval pressed.

"I had a contact who was going to set up a buy. If the supplier matched the photo of The Coyote we've got on file, I was set to take him down. My contact's name is on the file, but he won't deal with anyone he doesn't know. I spent months getting him to trust me."

"Maybe another detective can get in using your name."

Nick shook his head. "Too dangerous. Whoever takes over the case will need to build some street cred and work their way in."

Returning to Drew's side, Nick led her to the side door.

"From this point on, you're going to do exactly as I say," he snapped. "Follow my orders and we'll both stay alive."

"No problem—just as long as I happen to agree with what you're saying."

"My job's to make sure nobody snatches you, or worse. If I tell you to do something, do it."

It was that same no-negotiation tone her father and uncle had been famous for at home, and it made her bristle. She crossed her arms in front of her chest and glared at him. "We have something in common, Detective Blacksheep. I want to stay alive, and you want to keep me that way. But I won't be treated like an idiot. We'll work together to accomplish our mutual goal, but I'm not your subordinate, and never will be. Am I clear?"

"Perfectly. But here's the thing. When people are coming at you with fists or guns, there's no time for discussions," he said, glaring at her. "I'm trained to deal with life-and-death situations. You're not. If you want to live, do as you're told."

"I know the difference between an emergency and an insufferable ego. Do you?"

He muttered something incomprehensible under his breath.

She took a calming breath. "I get why you're angry, but don't take your frustrations out on me. There are a lot of women who'd probably be thrilled to let you take charge and follow in your footsteps, but I'm not one of them."

Nick ran an exasperated hand through his hair. So much for the sweet young thing he'd wanted to comfort. A day that had started off wrong was getting worse by the second.

"Wait right here—inside the building and away from the front entrance. I'm going to get my Jeep." It hadn't been a request, but he could see her weighing her options. "You want to avoid becoming an open target."

Accepting the logic, she nodded. "I tend to react very badly to people who give me orders, so think of me as an intelligent asset, not just an added responsibility."

"Stay here," Nick repeated, then hurried to where he'd left his Jeep. Unfortunately, he learned from one of the mechanics that his MDT had been sent to the shop to have the power supply replaced, so he'd have to do without it until a spare was located. He could have taken one of the department's unmarked cars, but they were all easily recognizable fleet vehicles.

Five minutes later they were headed west on Central Avenue, away from the city center. Pulling up to a stoplight, Nick looked around, always on alert mode while a sitting target.

"The arms dealer case sounded interesting. That Coyote person, do you think he lives in Three Rivers?" Drew asked, mostly to make conversation.

"I can't talk about an ongoing investigation," he said. "Especially someone else's."

"Are you going to stay in this foul mood forever?" she countered. "For the record, if I'd been given a choice, I wouldn't have chosen you either."

That was a first. He'd never had much of a problem with women, except for the ones who wanted a "relationship."

"Okay, I'll bite. If you'd had your choice, who would you have chosen? That crime-scene tech who went queasy carrying your purse? Or maybe you would have rather had by-the-book Koval."

"Actually, Nick, I wouldn't have picked a person at all. I'd have chosen a forty-five Colt, like my father carried, and found someone who could teach me how to use it."

He laughed out loud. "If it's any consolation, my nine millimeter SIG Sauer and I will be right by your side."

Drew adjusted her shoulder belt, then slipped her hands under her thighs. She hadn't been able to stop shaking since they'd left the station. "Something's not right," she said, looking through the rear window, then out the side mirror.

"What's up? Do you see something?"

"No, but I'm getting a very bad feeling—the creepy crawlies, you know?"

Nick glanced in the rearview mirror, and as he did, a sedan came out of a side street and drove up slowly. The driver eased forward, then casually pulled up beside them in the left-hand lane.

Nick glanced at the driver, but all he saw was a dark cap pulled low over the man's face. The man leaned over toward the open passenger-side window as if about to ask directions, then suddenly raised a pistol. "Stay away from Drew!" he yelled.

Nick stomped on the gas pedal at the same time he shoved Drew down on the seat. The Jeep roared into the intersection just as the man fired. Nick felt a thud behind his back as he swerved to his left, cutting off the shooter's car, then shifted gears and floored the Jeep.

Drew raised up slightly to look in her side mirror. "He's still back there, trying to come up on my side now."

"Stay down!" Nick pumped the brakes, then drew his handgun and looked to his right, ready to fire if the shooter pulled up even.

As the shooter's car swung wide left, crossing the center line, Nick also cut left, sliding around the corner and taking the cross street.

Slamming on the brakes this time, Nick pulled a one-eighty, sliding completely around in the road. Shifting down, he floored the pedal again and raced back to the intersection.

"Now we're on *your* tail," he muttered, concentrating on his next move.

The sedan had more horsepower than his Jeep and was pulling away. Steering with his left hand, Nick called police dispatch as he continued pursuit right into the warehouse district.

"We're going to lose him," Drew shouted, trying hard to keep the fleeing car in sight.

"No way." Nick shifted down.

The sedan took another right and Nick went after it, brushing a metal trash can that was spinning like a top after being struck by the sedan.

"Which way did he go?" Drew asked, when they reached the next street.

Nick screeched to a stop. "There," he pointed.

The city's largest municipal lot was straight ahead. Nick whipped out into the street and crossed over to the lot entrance.

An exit across the parking area showed at least three pairs of taillights going out.

"He's going out the other side," Drew said. "Can you back up and circle around?" Although she was terrified of actually catching up to the man, she was even more afraid of losing him.

Nick checked the mirror. A big pickup was now pulling out of a slot behind him. They were trapped in place.

"He's gone," Drew said, biting back tears of frustration. "We'll never catch up now."

Nick made the call to the station and put out an ATL, an attempt to locate. "You knew we were in trouble even before the shooter's car came into view. What keyed you to that?"

"I don't know. But I've learned never to ignore a feeling of impending danger." She jammed her hands into her coat, needing the warmth—inside and out.

Silence stretched out between them, and, noting the pallor of her face, he continued in a gentler voice. "For now, the man's gone and it's over. I doubt we'll get anywhere with that ATL. Based on past experiences, I'm betting that the car was probably stolen and will turn up abandoned somewhere, wiped clean of prints or destroyed by fire."

"But something odd's going on. There was only one guy in that car, not two like before. If both of them had come at us, they would have had a better chance to…kill us," she added in a strangled voice. "So what happened to the other man?"

"Maybe they figured that we'd be on the alert for two men. Or you might have left a mark on the one you slugged in the face that would have identified him."

"Where are we going now?"

"Back to the station. We need a debrief and a new plan. After the chief hears what just happened, he may decide that you're better off getting out of town altogether."

"This is turning out to be a very long night," Drew said, swallowing hard and slumping down in her seat.

Nick gave her a quick glance. Drew was holding on by a thread, but somehow, she wasn't falling apart. The librarian had turned out to be one helluva woman. "Keep in mind that you've come out ahead. You're alive, unhurt, and, if you face any more trouble, you've got the best backup in the state right next to you."

"You know what? I believe you," she murmured.

Though her words had been barely above a whisper, he heard her and smiled.

Chapter Four

As they rode back to the station, only the road noise from the Jeep's knobby tires marred the silence.

"Give me something to work with, Drew. Everyone makes enemies, and I need to know what I'm up against," Nick pressed.

"Everyone in *your* line of work makes enemies, but not in mine," she said. "I've wanted to work at the Willa Cather Public Library ever since high school," she said, softly. "Books have always been my first love. They saw me through the worst times of my life. I was only fifteen when my dad died unexpectedly. My mother never got over it, and followed him to the grave a year later. Uncle Earl took me in, but grieving for my parents was a long, hard process, and books gave me the only comfort I had. They transported me anywhere I wanted to be. Through them, I became a spy, a detective, and had adventures with elves and superheroes."

He'd never been one for fancy daydreams, but adventures with *elves?* He glanced out the window so she couldn't see him smiling.

"As I got older I knew I wanted a job that would help me guide others into that safe world where imagination was king. That's why I became a librarian. To be offered a position in the place that started it all for me was like icing on the cake. But things haven't exactly gone as I'd planned."

"What about your competitors for the job? Anyone with hard feelings there?"

"Nick, think about it. Librarians don't hire hit men."

As they pulled into the station's underground parking garage, Nick climbed out, then stopped and examined his side of the Jeep. There was a single bullet hole in the side panel just behind his door. The round had passed through, entering the back of his seat. There was no exit hole, so the round was probably still inside the upholstery.

Seeing Earl Simmons standing by the stairwell door, Nick hurried over with Drew. "Anything on the shooter?" Nick asked.

Though Earl held the door open for Drew, he never even glanced at her. "We've already located the shooter's vehicle. It was stolen," he told Nick. "The crime scene people are on their way now."

"There's a round lodged in the driver's-side back rest somewhere," Nick said. "I accelerated just before he squeezed the trigger."

Captain Wright strode down the hall toward them. "What the heck happened, Blacksheep?"

Chief Franklin came around the corner just then. "Let's go into my office and talk about this."

They all gathered inside the chief's office. Earl Simmons had come in as well, followed by Detective Harry Koval, who closed the door behind him as Nick and Drew caught everyone up to date.

"Is it possible the shooter followed you from the station?" Captain Wright asked.

"I kept watch and saw no one, so I can't tell you how he pulled it off," Nick said. "But here's what I do know. Drew saw something I missed. I don't know how, but she knew that something wasn't right *before* the attempted hit went down."

Drew sighed as all eyes turned to her. She'd been through

this before with the men in her family. Police officers preferred to deal with tangible concepts, and woman's intuition didn't qualify. Intending to give it her best shot anyway, she answered the questions in their eyes. "Have any of you ever known that someone was behind you without turning around? Or maybe had the feeling the phone was going to ring, and it did?"

"No," came the unanimous reply.

"All right. Let's try this from a different angle. Think of your experiences out in the field—like maybe a time when you knew a suspect was going to bolt, or reach for his weapon, even though he hadn't moved."

"Feelings like those are usually based on something concrete, like a change of expression, or a flicker of movement," Nick said. "They're explainable. Think back and concentrate. What triggered the feeling you got in the car?"

Drew sighed. They had to have it in black and white, but intuition was intangible and didn't work that way. Still, she closed her eyes and tried her best. "The streets were almost empty. I was looking ahead at the path cut by the Jeep's headlights when I began to feel uneasy. I looked in the rearview mirror, and that's when I saw the sedan behind us. After it closed in, everything went crazy."

"The shooter yelled, telling me to stay away from Drew," Nick said. "He knew her name."

"I heard him clearly, too, but I didn't recognize the voice," Drew said.

"So we're back to the stalker angle," Chief Franklin said. "The shooter is jealous and possessive, but you still have no idea who he is?"

"No, I don't," Drew answered.

Wright looked at Nick. "You should start wearing a vest, Nick. You, too, Ms. Simmons."

"From what you've said, Blacksheep, it appears the gunman had a plan." Koval's slow, methodical voice held everyone's attention. "To stay ahead of him we'll have to come up with a better one. We can start by having me cover the outside of whatever place you stay at tonight. Tomorrow, we'll see where the investigation leads."

"I'll be happy to cooperate fully," Drew said, mostly to remind everyone that she *did* have a say in the matter, "but we never made it to my place earlier and I'll need to pick up a few things. I live in a gated apartment complex, so it should be safe enough to stop by there for a few minutes."

Koval shook his head. "No way. You'll have to rough it for now."

They left the room and Nick pointed to a room with a re-inforced metal door. "We need to stop at the armory and get some vests for both of us."

After putting on the vests they went down to the garage. This time Nick was able to pick up an MDT from a mechanic. Returning with Drew to his Jeep, he plugged the computer into the accessory jack and they got underway.

Noting how anxious she was, Nick gave her a smile. "Relax. Koval's nearby, ready to provide backup if we need it. There are other units in the area, too, still searching for the van."

"It's bad enough that someone's after me, but now I'm putting others in harm's way. I wish I could just stay somewhere that's one hundred percent safe until this is over."

He smiled gently. "Like the fortress cave of a superhero?" he said, thinking of what she'd said about books.

"Why not?" she answered, with a sad smile.

"I have no cave, but I'm a good shot, and I'm darned good at my job. Nothing's going to happen to you, Drew."

"I've slipped through death's grasp twice now, but it's not done with me yet."

"What you're going through happens to everyone who comes face-to-face with their own mortality. Staring death in the eye—that changes a person."

"Including you?" she asked, looking directly at him.

He nodded. "I was in the Marine Corps, and I saw my share of combat. My nightmares are a lot worse than the average cop's." He said nothing for several long moments, then glanced at her and gave her a totally outrageous grin. "Of course, that's because I'm badder than most of the guys in the PD."

She laughed. "Is that because you're an ex-Marine?"

"There's no such thing. I'm a *former* Marine. Once a Marine, always a Marine." He took a breath, then, after a moment, added, "No matter what lies ahead, I want you to remember one thing. I make a very good friend, Drew, and a very bad enemy—as the ones after you will soon find out if they don't back off."

"All I want is to live through this so I can go back to my nice, quiet life," she said.

He nodded but didn't say anything. Experience told him that it could be a long time before Drew's life became either nice or quiet again.

Chapter Five

They drove to the outskirts of town and eventually arrived at a tired-looking one-story cinder block motel along the old highway. The bright neon sign at the front looked as worn as the rest of the place, its letters advertising the QU-LITY -OTEL.

"You're kidding. You want to spend a night in this roach trap?"

"It's better inside. I guarantee you'll have a clean room and hot running water."

"And will we share?"

He gave her a slow grin. "Rooms? Beds? The first, for sure, as for the other...if that was an invitation..."

She nearly choked. "No, it was a legitimate question. I'm not sure how this is supposed to work. We take turns sleeping?"

"Leave those details to me," he said, glancing around, then added, "Wait here."

As he walked to the entrance, she watched the way he moved, advancing with purposeful strides, more like a soldier than a cop. There was an edge to him that practically dared anyone to stand in his way.

He returned a moment later and opened her door. "It's clear. Let's go."

As she stepped out of the Jeep their eyes met, and for a

moment she forgot to breathe. Nick had a lean, powerful build that could make any sane woman's mouth water, but it was his eyes that attracted her most. They were nearly black in the dim parking lot lights, and impossible to read. Mystery clung to him like a second skin.

Drew grabbed her book bag and purse, then followed Nick into the lobby and to the front desk. The young Navajo man there greeted Nick with an enthusiastic smile. *"Yáat'ééh,"* he called, using the Navajo expression for hello. "It's good to see you, man."

"You *didn't* see me," Nick said.

"No problem. What's up?" he said, giving Drew a quick once-over.

"I'm looking for adjoining rooms, somewhere toward the middle of the building, a place with one way in and one way out."

"You'll need one of our family suites then," he said, placing a numbered key on the table in front of Nick. "Down the hall and to the left. If there's anything else I can do for you, just let me know."

"Dinner—anything at all—would be great," he said, putting two twenties on the counter.

"Hey, for that amount I'll even throw in a continental breakfast with plenty of java. Seven in the morning okay?"

"Sure," Nick said.

As they walked down the long hall, Drew was surprised to see that everything was meticulously clean. There was no sign of dust anywhere, including the top of the ice machine.

Almost as if sensing her thoughts, Nick spoke. "I know Joe Tso. Though the place isn't much to look at from the outside, he's got great plans for it." Nick paused, then added, "Joe's a member of my clan."

"Navajos are never really alone in the world, are they?" she asked, with a touch of envy.

"No, not really. We have our families, our clans, our tribe. It's all part of who we are."

That sense of connectedness was something she hadn't felt since the death of her parents. Although she'd lived with her aunt and uncle, they never really made room for her in their lives. She'd felt more like a tenant. Yet something good had come out of that. She learned to rely on herself. The lessons she'd learned had given her the strength to pursue her own dreams.

Nick stopped halfway down the hall and unlocked the door.

Drew followed him inside and looked around. They had one large bedroom, an open passage minus a door, and a second, smaller bedroom. Both had their own bathrooms.

"It may not be perfect, but we're safe here," Nick said. "Anyone trying to get to you will have to go through me."

Drew checked out the smaller bedroom with the two twin beds, and peeked inside the bathroom. "An old-fashioned claw-footed tub! I love it! This is definitely my room." She sat her purse and backpack on the table.

"Then it's settled."

Drew glanced through the open door and knew that she'd be sleeping with her clothes on tonight. Anything else would be tempting fate.

Nick strode around both rooms like a panther on the prowl, checking everything. "Everything's clear and in good order. I'm going to get a few things from the Jeep. Lock up behind me."

She did as he asked, then sat on the edge of Nick's bed as she waited for him to return. To think that this morning had started just like any other day! Now, here she was sharing adjoining rooms with a man who was equal parts trouble and temptation.

She was still contemplating a long soak when she heard someone walk up to the door and stop. Thinking it was Nick, she waited for the sound of the key in the lock, but nothing happened. Fear, sudden and overwhelming, engulfed her. For a moment she couldn't move.

"*Yáat'ééh,*" Joe Tso called out. "It's me, from the front desk. I've got your dinner, but no free hands to knock."

"Hang on." She opened the door and invited Joe in. Hearing more footsteps, Drew glanced out and saw Nick coming down the hall carrying a gym bag and a rolled-up blanket she suspected contained his shotgun.

"Your favorite, cuz," the young Navajo man said, as Nick came in, then placed two greasy paper bags on the table.

Once Joe left, they sat down by the table and brought out two huge, foil-wrapped enchiladas, still warm. He placed one in front of her and quickly unwrapped the other and took a huge mouthful.

Drew unwrapped hers and took a bite. "These are heavenly," she said.

Hungry, they ate quickly. Drew smiled at him as she consumed the last bite. "That's the best dinner I've had in ages," she said, licking the salsa off each of her fingers.

Nick watched her for a moment, then swallowed the last of the cold water in the bottle. "Will you help me get out of this vest? An old injury I got overseas is acting up. I aggravated it earlier today when my brother and I were working out. The vest made it worse."

Drew helped him remove his vest, and as she did, his western style shirt came open in front, revealing the jagged scars that covered his upper chest. "Those aren't bullet wounds, are they?"

He shook his head. "Shrapnel—flying metal."

She ran a gentle finger over one of the scars and heard him suck in his breath. As she looked up at him, his eyes, gleaming like granite, held hers.

Her mouth went dry. He was magnificent in every sense of the word. Instead of detracting from his looks, the toll war had taken on his body enhanced his appeal. He looked rugged, a man of experience, whose assurance came from self-knowledge, not bravado.

"If you don't need any more help," she managed.

"I need *you*," he whispered. "Don't go so soon."

A shiver touched her spine, and for a second she stood where she was, feeling the heat from his body and wanting more. "You're on duty...."

"Koval's outside in the parking lot, and he'll be there till daybreak. Joe's keeping an eye on things, too. We're okay," he said gently, then cupped her cheek with his palm, and traced her lips with his thumb. "Let's get to know each other a little better."

Awareness and desire squeezed the air from her lungs. She had to use every last shred of willpower she possessed just to step away. "You and I are temporary associates—partners by necessity. Let's keep it that way."

He reached for her hand and brought it up to his lips, kissing the pulse point there. "Your heartbeat tells me a different story."

Drew tried to swallow, but her mouth was completely dry. "What we may want right now and what we really need are two very different things."

"I can make them be one and the same," he said, leaning over and whispering the words in her ear.

A shiver coursed through her, but once again she found the will to step back. "*Stop it.* I'm no one's one-night stand. Your reputation precedes you, Detective Blacksheep." Without another word, she walked into her room and unhooked the straps of her own vest. After slipping out of the heavy garment, she turned on the TV and sat cross-legged on the edge of the mattress.

"You're not fooling anyone," he murmured.

Drew pretended not to hear. Just standing close to him had made everything inside her blossom to life. He was the stuff of dreams. To make love for the first time and have it be to a man like Nick... She sighed.

As her heart slowed to almost normal, she glanced at the tub wistfully. There was no way she was going to take off her clothes now. She knew her limitations.

NICK WENT STRAIGHT INTO the shower and turned on the cold water. He wasn't used to being turned down. He wasn't a traditionalist, but like them, he believed that the Anglo world made too much of sex. It was a pleasurable need—like eating, only better.

Making love—that was something else entirely. It meant a deeper union—a coming together of two halves, a completion. Experience told him that was precisely what a woman like Drew would require.

As he allowed the cold water to course over his body, unsatisfied needs pounded through him. He should have taken off his own vest, but watching her lick her fingertips had stirred something inside him. He'd wanted her. And she'd wanted him. He'd felt her tremble and had heard the little hitch in her breath. Yet something had stopped her.

Innocence? Could that be part of the answer? Maybe she'd never had a man, not in that way. The possibility made his body harden again, but this time it came with a hefty dose of guilt. He had to keep his distance from her. If she was saving herself for a future husband, that left him out of the running. He wasn't marriage material.

Nick came out of the shower, toweled himself dry, then pulled on his jeans. As he walked barefoot into his room, he looked through the open doorway and saw that Drew had fallen asleep on the small bed.

Good. One less distraction to worry about.

He used his phone to check with Koval next, and after getting the all-clear, he crossed the room and unwrapped his shotgun from the blanket. Placing the weapon back on the bed, safety on, he sat down at the table, brought out his pistol, and began cleaning it.

Although he'd tried to be quiet, the click of the slide woke her and Drew sat up immediately.

"It's okay, relax." Nick stood and placed his pistol back in its holster. "I'm going to take a walk outside and make sure everything's secure."

Nick left the room and walked down the hall. As he stepped out into the parking lot, the cold night air rushed to greet him. He remained close to the wall, in the shadows. He liked the freedom of the night, that's why he'd embraced investigative work. He belonged in the darkness, just as someone like Drew belonged in the light.

Chapter Six

Drew woke up early the next morning. She hadn't slept well. Although she'd pretended to be asleep, she'd been aware of Nick's every move. She'd seen him walking around, occasionally returning to his bed, only to get back up again.

"I'm glad you're awake, it's time for us to get going," he said.

Drew watched him slip the badge onto his belt, then adjust his holster and put on his jacket, hiding the weapon from view. The entire process was effortless and without any wasted motion—the mark of a true professional. Everything about him spoke of confidence and a fierce devotion to his job. Law enforcement was as much a part of him as the beat of his heart.

Her father and uncle had been the same way. They'd always stood ready to meet any challenge, and even sacrifice their lives, if need be. Yet, it was their wives who'd paid the highest price. She remembered her mother and her aunt spending countless nights worrying and waiting for their husbands to come home. They'd paced and prayed, fear their constant companion.

Drew had learned one thing back then: the man in her future would have to be someone with a nice, predictable, nine-to-five job.

"Koval's off the clock now, so I'm going to take a look

outside. Joe should be coming around with breakfast soon, but don't open the door to anyone except him or me."

SHORTLY AFTER HE LEFT, she heard a soft knock at the door, followed by the word, "breakfast." Drew opened the door and, in an instant, realized her mistake. A cart slammed into her middle, tossing her backwards against the table. She bounced against it, then fell to the floor.

The man wearing the ski mask came toward her, holding a Taser in his hand.

Drew screamed and shoved the wheeled cart against him.

The man grunted as the cart pinned him against the door-frame, but with a mighty shove, he pushed it away.

Drew saw the shotgun on the bed, half wrapped in a blanket, but knew she'd never be able to reach it in time.

Just as the man raised his Taser, she heard footsteps in the hall.

"Nick!" she screamed, then realized her mistake a heartbeat later.

Her attacker whirled and fired the Taser, sending Nick to the floor, wracked with pain.

Joe, right behind Nick, tackled the man and tore the Taser from his hand, yanking the contacts off Nick's legs. Drew grabbed the shotgun, but their assailant ran out of the room before she could take aim.

Groggy but no longer in pain, and aware that the footsteps down the hall had faded, Nick used his cell phone to call for backup.

Nick glared at Drew. "I told you *not* to open the door to anyone except Joe and me."

"I thought it *was* Joe." Drew took a deep breath, then let it out slowly, forcing herself to calm down as she placed the shotgun back on the blanket. "I made a mistake, but we've now learned something new." Forcing herself to use the coolly logical tone of voice she knew he'd understand, she continued. "You need to figure out who leaked our location. We weren't followed. You and I made sure of that."

"You're right," Nick said.

Drew watched him. Nick didn't like to lose, and there was something dark and deadly in his gaze as he shifted his focus to the Taser lying on the floor.

"Don't touch anything," he told them. "My backup will be here shortly. Joe, go wait for him and tell him where we are."

Joe nodded and hurried out the door.

"You say you can sense danger, but this time you had no vibes warning you?" Nick asked, stretching his arms and legs, trying to shake off the aftereffects of the Taser.

"I was...distracted," she said, at last, still feeling guilty about what had happened. He was right to be angry. She should have been paying more attention, not daydreaming. Yet Nick held the same fascination for her as a force of nature. Being around him was a bit like standing out in a clearing during the middle of a storm and watching lightning flash across the sky. The intensity, the wildness, mesmerized—yet there was always the danger of being struck.

They heard running footsteps, then Koval appeared at the door, breathing hard. "What the heck happened? I've only been gone a half hour and things are falling apart already."

"There was a screwup," Nick snapped. "Add to that the fact somebody tipped off the bad guy to our location."

"Let's focus on the details of what just went down," Koval said, looking at the Taser. "The suspect obviously came prepared. Take out the security, nab the target. This wasn't a hit, it was a botched kidnaping."

"There was only one man, at least I only saw the one. But he knew which room I was in, and the timing suggests that he also knew Nick had stepped out," Drew said.

"We need to go over the list of people who knew we were here," Nick said.

"I knew, so did Captain Wright and the chief. It was also information I had to add to the department payment vouchers so we could cover your stay," Koval said. "I set that in motion last night while I was outside on surveillance. But that's all internal department business and is supposed to be secure."

"We need new tactics," Nick said. "But first, let's work the scene and see what else we can find."

"No. Wait for the team," Koval ordered, turning as Joe appeared in the doorway.

"There's no time to play things by the book, Koval. It's possible that someone planted a bug on me or Drew. If that's the case, we need to find the tracking device *now*. Otherwise, we'll just lead them to our next location."

Nick motioned toward her big handbag. "Would you do the honors?"

It hadn't been a question, but at least he'd asked instead of ordered. She dumped the contents of the tote onto the table.

Nick checked her wallet, her hairbrush handle, and felt along the sides of her purse. "There's nothing here."

Koval, who'd been searching their trash, shook his head. "Nor here."

Nick went through his own gear, and looked up at Joe. "Did you tell anyone that you'd seen me? Think hard before you answer."

"I don't have to, bro. I never told anyone who the food was for and I didn't use your name on the register. I checked you in as Hosteen Shibuddy."

Nick smiled. It was Nava-glish, a combination of Navajo and English that meant Mr. My Friend.

"My stuff is clean," he said, zipping the gym bag shut.

"And my backpack, too," Drew added, beginning to put her references back into the zippered compartments.

Once the crime scene team arrived, Drew took her book

bag while Nick picked up his gear. Together they returned to his Jeep.

"Where are we going?" she asked, climbing in as he locked the shotgun back in place.

"To the station."

She considered it for several moments. "You're going to try and get permission to operate independently and not report our location to anyone. Am I right?"

"You read minds, too?"

"No, but it stands to reason. Something or someone gave our location away. Koval… Do you trust him? This happened after he left this morning, which suggests he could have given the intruder an all-clear signal to make his move."

"I don't like the man any more than he does me, but he's a good cop, and I trust him to have my back in a tight spot."

"So what's the problem between you two?" she asked.

"The trouble between Koval and me isn't the result of any one incident. We just have different ways of working, and we annoy the heck out of each other. I think Koval's methods don't leave any room for independent thought. He would probably tell you that I'm a loose cannon, and it's a miracle my cases stack up in court."

"You just have opposite ways of accomplishing the same thing."

"We were lucky we didn't pound each other's faces into the ground," he said.

A few minutes later, Nick pulled into the station's underground garage. "Chief Franklin is going to fight the possibility that someone in his department is playing both sides of the fence. I expect they'll put us in different rooms and grill us long and hard, looking for possible leads."

"Let them," she answered. "No one wants them to find answers more than I do. I want my life back."

As they entered through the basement access, Koval and another officer met them in the hall. Koval took Nick aside as the other detective introduced himself to Drew. "I'm Detective Marty Sandoval. I'm going to need to search your purse, Ms. Simmons, and that backpack."

"That's already been done, Detective."

"Not by me," came his reply.

She'd just turned her purse and book bag over to Sandoval when Koval came over. "The chief is speaking to Blacksheep right now. While they're busy, would you come with me?"

Moments later, Koval and Drew were in a room at the end of the hall. She was almost sure that the mirror, which ran the length of one wall, was one-way glass.

"I want you to catch this person, or people, who've been turning my life into a circus," she said, before he could speak. "How can I help you do that?"

He smiled slowly. "You hate giving up control of your own life, don't you?"

"Yes, I do," she answered, honestly.

"I don't blame you," he said. "So let's work together and see what we can come up with."

NICK SAT ACROSS FROM Chief Franklin's desk. "I know we weren't followed, sir. There's only one explanation for what happened. Someone gave away our location. We have a leak."

"That can't be right." Franklin's face hardened and his voice dropped almost an octave. "It looks to me like you screwed up again by failing to spot a tail."

Nick shook his head. "Koval and me both? Not this time—and not before, either."

"And you're one hundred percent sure of that?" Chief Franklin demanded.

"Nothing's impossible, but I'd stake my job on it. And if I'm right, there's only one way to insure her safety. Give me complete autonomy. I don't report my whereabouts to anyone, and I make my own decisions without having to go through channels."

Chief Franklin leaned back and regarded him thoughtfully. "In the long run, that could end up leaving you more exposed than you are now. That could be fatal to Drew Simmons—and yourself."

"My plan isn't without risk, but I believe the woman and I will be safest that way."

"Bring Ms. Simmons in here and let's see what she's got to say about it," Chief Franklin said.

Nick hadn't expected this response, but did as the chief asked. A few minutes later, he led Drew into the room. Koval accompanied them, having insisted on it.

The chief updated them on what he and Nick had discussed. "Ms. Simmons, I'd like you to consider all sides of this issue before telling us what you think. You'd be out there without backup, and as you've already seen, things can go wrong in a hurry."

Drew gave Nick a worried look. "I could see you telling only one person where we're at, but no one at all?" She shook her head. "That doesn't seem like such a good idea either."

"I'd hand-pick the ones I take into my confidence," Nick said. "If there's still a leak, I'll know who it is."

Koval cleared his throat, and all eyes turned to him. "There's something else we need to consider. The suspect's goal isn't to kill Drew, not with the van, and not this morning. If it had been, he would have come armed with more than a Taser."

"Maybe the Taser was meant to disable Nick," Drew said, then taking a shaky breath, continued. "To kill me is one thing, but killing a cop is a whole different game. That brings every agency around down on the criminal."

Chief Franklin nodded. "She's got a point, Blacksheep. You assumed that the suspect knew you were out of the room and timed things just right. But that may not be the case."

For several seconds, no one spoke. Finally, Nick broke the silence. "Drew should make a list of all the casual contacts she sees daily—everyone from the guy who bags her groceries to the one she says hello to when she picks up her mail. We may get a hit on someone with a record."

"I can do that," Drew said.

"I'd also like to do something a bit riskier before taking her back into hiding with me. Using backup, I want to go with her to the mall at the same time she normally does her shopping. Then I'll tail her as she goes about her business. If we keep to her schedule, we're going to encounter the staff and regular shoppers who are usually there at that time. Maybe we can push the guy who stalked her before into coming out into the open."

"That's not half bad, as far as plans go," Koval said, grudgingly.

WORKING WITH NICK, DREW managed to compile the list he'd wanted of people she saw daily, though she didn't know many of their names.

"The ones on that list are just ordinary people," she said as Koval and Nick studied it. "Take the guy I buy the newspaper from, for example. He's always outside the grocery store. He's disabled and works harder than anyone else I know just to get by. Then there's the guy who lives in the apartment across from mine. John something. He's always trying to make small talk, but he's far more interested in computers than in me. He and his buddy hang out together and spend most weekends and evenings playing video games, judging from what I've seen and heard. I've also been doing temp work at city hall, and there are a bunch of male employees who always say hello." She paused, then with a scowl, added, "The only one who's an all-out creep is Richard Beck."

"Fire Marshal Beck?" Nick asked, recognizing the name.

"Yeah. He comes by city hall on occasion. The guy's a jerk who won't take no for an answer."

"But none of the people on your list is the guy you saw at the mall?" Koval pressed.

"I don't think so, but remember that I purposely avoided looking directly at him, and never got close."

As Koval walked off, Nick stared at the list on the computer screen. "I'd like to do a little more work on these names and cross-reference them with our databases, especially the sex offender list."

"You could have kept that part to yourself," Drew muttered, then in a normal tone of voice, added, "This would be a good time for me to go talk to Beth," she said, noting that Beth had chosen to remain on the ground floor rather than go to her private office.

As Nick focused on the computer search, Drew walked across the big room to the records department, situated behind a glass partition.

"Hi, Beth," she greeted, pulling up a chair. "How are you feeling today?"

Beth gave her a weary smile. "It's getting harder to hold a full-time job and take care of Charlie. But it's worse for him."

"I'm so sorry."

"Things will get better," she said, forcing a smile. "Once I take a leave of absence, I'll be able to concentrate on him full time."

"I'm going to be here for a while. Is there anything I can do to help you today?"

"Why don't you get started updating some of these records?" Beth asked, pointing to some file folders. "Now that we've switched to the new system, these old but still active files have to be reentered in a format that's compatible with the new software."

As Drew got down to work, she glanced over at Nick, but

he seemed totally absorbed in the work he was doing at his terminal.

"Having Nick as a bodyguard probably rates as the number-one fantasy around here. A lot of women in this department are green with envy," Beth whispered to Drew. "But be real careful around him, honey. He's strictly a love 'em and leave 'em kind of guy. You can forget anything beyond a few memorable evenings—so I've been told."

Drew nodded. "Nick's trouble, all right, and he's definitely not for me. Corny as it sounds, I'm saving myself for that one special person. But I'm not ready to even think about settling down. I like being single and answering to no one but myself. And if I ever do marry, I can guarantee you that it won't be to someone who's always telling me what to do."

"You and Nick have something in common, then. If there ever was a free spirit, it's him."

"He's easy on the eyes, but wanting is often better than getting." Drew stole a look at Nick, then focused back on the screen. If she kept that thought in mind, she'd do just fine.

AFTER RESEARCHING FORMER Chief Simmons, Nick looked Drew's name up on Google and found several newspaper articles dating back to the death of her parents. She'd been left a sizable inheritance. Maybe she'd become a kidnap-for-ransom target. Yet, her lifestyle didn't reflect great wealth. Case in point—her car. Maybe she'd lost most of her money in the recent stock market decline.

Nick leaned back in his chair and considered everything he'd learned. Drew's independent streak was no doubt a product of her past, and wouldn't make her easy to protect. But they had more in common than he'd realized. He knew what it was like to have everything that defined you suddenly taken away. When life dealt you a hand like that, lifelong scars remained. Like him, Drew had become a fighter to survive; but this time she was out of her league.

Nick felt the weight of the badge clipped to his belt. He was good at what he did. No one would touch her.

Almost as if sensing his gaze on her, Drew turned her head and gave him a tentative smile.

Nick stood and was about to walk over when Koval came into the room. Catching their attention, the detective gestured for them to join him.

"I've got things set up for your trip to the mall this evening." Koval went over the details of his arrangement with mall security, then added, "Drew, I understand that for you this is personal, but stay calm tonight and don't worry, you'll have double coverage."

She nodded, but "calm" was the last thing she felt.

"What time do you normally arrive at the mall?" Koval asked.

"Around seven."

"When you're set to arrive, give me a call, Blacksheep. I'll keep an eye on both of you from a distance. In the meantime, the chief wants to meet with us one last time."

Koval headed down the hall but Nick hung back and pulled her to one side. "I want you to know one thing. They'll never get past me again," he growled. "I'll die first."

Truth and determination rang through his words. "I believe you," she whispered.

Chapter Seven

Chief Franklin waved them all to a seat. "Now that you've had a chance to review new information, have you come up with any new theories, detectives?"

"There's a possible motive for the kidnaping attempts that we haven't considered before," Nick said. "A monetary one."

"You're referring to the life insurance money my father and mother left me. It was listed, incorrectly I might add, in a newspaper article that came out after their deaths," Drew said. "The amount I got wasn't in the midsix figures, not even close. What I got was a trust fund that gave me the ability to pay for college and help me weather rough patches. But that's about it."

"I read the article, too," Koval said, with a nod. "Maybe someone else, who was misinformed, decided they want what's left."

"That's a real old article," Drew reminded them, "and my lifestyle isn't opulent. I'm working two jobs."

Nick looked at Drew and held her gaze. "If you were asked to come up with a theory for what's going on, what would it be?"

Drew considered it for a long time. "I don't think they want to kill me. Maybe it's like you suggested. They just want me out of the way for some reason. But I can't believe they're going through all this trouble because they want the librarian post the city promised me, or my temp job here."

"Stalkers don't always act according to logic," Koval said. "It could be someone who thought that the way you smiled and said good morning meant you'd be together forever. The way I figure it, none of this is going to make sense until we get a fix on whoever's responsible and see the whole picture from his point of view."

"But I encounter a lot of people throughout the course of a day, Detective Koval," she protested.

"Which is why I'm going to start with your neighbors, and go down the list you gave us," Koval said.

"So, when will I be able to go home?" Drew asked.

"Let us continue this investigation for the next twenty-four hours, then we'll see where we stand," Captain Wright said.

Moments later, Nick and Drew left the chief's office and headed down the hall toward the parking garage. "We might get lucky tonight, and this whole thing could be over for you in a matter of hours."

She saw his expression harden and felt his mood shift. "You're hoping for a confrontation. That's *your* kind of operation," she said, knowing that she was reading him right.

"True. I've always preferred to face an enemy head-on."

"I hope he comes after me this evening, too," she admitted, in a whisper-thin voice. "I want this to be over. I don't want to be afraid anymore."

DREW GLANCED AROUND THEM as they drove through downtown. "Where are we going?"

"How about if I take you to my house—well, my brother's, too. It's out in the sticks and almost impossible to approach without being seen. Neither of us likes surprises."

Caution screamed at her to make Nick choose someplace else. Yet, the temptation to learn more about the man by her side was too strong to resist, and his home would tell her more about him than words ever could.

The drive took them west out of the city, then north up a narrow river valley flanked by tall mesas and steep canyons.

The afternoon sun was shining brightly, and warmth radiated off the rocky walls of the cliffs, as the valley narrowed. There was no sign of civilization here.

"I would have thought you would have chosen someplace more…populated. That way, if you got into trouble, your fellow officers would be nearby," she said.

"I don't live alone. So, basically I've got all the company I can stand," he teased.

He soon turned off the road onto a small drive lined with gravel.

"The man you were investigating…this Coyote person. Do you think he would come after you even though you're a police officer?"

"In a heartbeat," he answered.

"How do you sleep, knowing that there are people out there who'd jump at the chance to get you? I'm having a hard time dealing with the fact that two men are after me. The fear never really goes away."

"Maintaining the balance between good and evil takes work, but if good sits back, evil runs unchecked. That's based on Navajo Way teachings, but it's also common sense."

Maybe this kind of lifestyle was right for him, but she hated every second of it. It was a horrible nightmare come to life. Rather than waiting patiently for the library position to open up so she could follow her dream, she was now running for her life.

How had things suddenly become so crazy? She'd never been one for adventure. She wanted a nice, quiet, predictable life—qualities she'd never known growing up. Now here she was, involved in a high-stakes investigation, where one wrong move could mean death.

"Fate always has the last word, doesn't it?" she whispered.

"I've learned the hard way never to count on anything except for the here and now." He parked in a circle of gravel where the road came to a dead end. "Welcome to my place."

She could see nothing ahead except thick junipers, sandstone boulders, and an empty arroyo. "You live underground, or do you camp out?"

"No, it's right through those junipers. We bought that old ranch house after we left the Corps. The place is perfect for two cops who plan to remain bachelors for life," he said with a grin. As they got out, he added, "Watch out for Crusher."

"I beg your pardon?"

"He's a dog the size of a horse, and he has the run of the property. He looks a little intimidating, but he's not mean, so don't worry," he said. "Someone dumped the mutt on the side of the highway back at the turnoff one night, and Travis picked him up after he wandered into the beam of his headlights." He grinned at her. "My brother's the softie in the family."

"I'll be sure to tell him you said that when I meet him."

Nick burst out laughing. "Let's go."

He led the way up a rocky pathway. As they came to the end of the trail, she saw what looked to be a large cabin—or lodge. The house was made of pine logs, and with the green metal roof, it fit into the hillside as naturally as the trees around it.

"My brother may have kept Crusher inside. The ground's still damp from a cold rain we had the other night, and the dog tends to track in tons of mud." He unlocked the front door, stepped in front of her, and led the way inside.

"I thought you said the dog wasn't mean," she said quickly.

"He's not," he said, then glanced back at her. "Are you

worried because I came in first, or do you think I'm just rude?" Seeing her hesitate, he grinned. "Navajo men are taught to enter a room before a woman does. I know Anglo men have the opposite custom—ladies first—but we look at it a little differently. If there's danger, the man should be the one to face it, instead of sending the woman ahead as cannon fodder."

She laughed. "I never thought of it that way."

Drew suddenly heard what sounded like the two-beat stride of a galloping horse, then a moment later, a giant black dog, with the jowls of a mastiff and the body of a bear, rushed out of an adjoining room. He crashed into Nick, rocking him back on his boot heels.

The beast must have weighed a hundred and fifty pounds, but Nick lifted it off the ground in a giant hug. "Hey, Crusher." He set the dog down, wrestled the stuffed toy from its mouth, and threw it back down the hall.

The whole scene was so unlike the dark, dangerous warrior she'd spent time with, she had to laugh.

A few seconds later, another Navajo man entered through the backdoor of the house and walked into the kitchen. He was a little taller than Nick, and wore a leather pouch at his belt, next to his holster. A small fetish hung from his neck on a leather string. As he got close, she recognized the carving of a hawk. The dog greeted him instantly and enthusiastically.

"This is my brother. He follows the ways of our tribe, so we'll avoid using his name," Nick said.

"Names aren't allowed? Why? Do you mind if I ask?"

Travis answered her. "Names have power that belongs to their bearer. Using a name too often is said to drain that strength."

As she looked at the two brothers side-by-side, she noted that there wasn't much of a physical resemblance between them, except their high cheekbones. But they definitely had other things in common. They both had an air of unshakable confidence—and the physical attributes and intelligent eyes to back it up.

"Hey, Crusher, I brought you a present," Travis said, fondly, bending down and giving the animal a knotted rawhide bone.

"His name doesn't count?" Drew asked.

"Crusher's his nickname. His real name's a secret," Travis replied, grinning, then glanced at his brother. "So, what are your plans?"

"We're going to spend the night here," Nick said.

"Roger that. I've got the graveyard shift tonight, so you'll have the place to yourselves. But don't worry. Crusher will make sure you don't get any unexpected company."

"Are you sticking around for a while, or taking off again?" Nick asked.

"I'm heading back to town. I'm meeting one of my informants." Travis left and they heard the front door slam and click shut.

"Let me give you a quick tour," Nick said. He led Drew down the hall and into a large room that had been converted into a well-equipped gym. It held everything from boxing training equipment to floor mats, a weight bench, and at least three hundred pounds of barbells and weights.

"My brother and I like to stay in shape," he said, following her gaze.

"You've succeeded admirably," she said, then realized she'd spoken out loud. "I mean, I can see you're both in good shape."

He grinned slowly.

The purely masculine gesture tore through her like a jolt of electricity. She looked away and pretended to be fascinated by his gym equipment. Not that she was fooling anyone. He knew precisely how he affected her.

Drew strolled to the door, then glanced back at Nick. "Where to next?"

He led her to the end of the hall and showed her his room. It was sparse—nothing hung on the honey-colored log walls. The full-size oak bed in the middle was neatly made, but there was no bedspread.

"No photos," she said, casually glancing at the walls.

"Other than my brother, there's very little about my past that I want to remember."

She gave him a surprised look, but he shook his head, signaling her to drop it. Reluctantly accepting his request, she did.

Next, Nick showed her Travis's room. There were several fetishes dusted with pollen on the dresser, but little else.

As they passed through the hall again, Drew slowed down to take one more glance at the gym. Then, on the spur of the moment, she went inside. She walked to the heavy boxing bag, lifted one hand, and gave it a light punch. The bag didn't even move.

"I know men work their problems out on these things, but it doesn't seem very satisfying," she said. "Maybe if you put in one of those voice boxes so it would scream when you hit it…"

He laughed and came closer. "The problem is that you didn't really punch it. You tapped it. But considering the way you make a fist, that was probably a good thing."

"A fist is a fist," she said, raising her curled hand. "What are you talking about?"

"If you curl your fingers around your thumb like that, you'll end up breaking or dislocating the bone." He took her hand in both of his and curled her fingers while holding her thumb out. "Now curb your thumb around the outside of your fist, so that the tip of your thumb touches the middle joint of your ring finger," he said. "Like this," he added, demonstrating.

She tried to focus on his instructions, not the way his touch had made everything inside her soften and yearn for more.

Forcing herself to concentrate, she stood inches from the bag, bent her wrist and tapped it again.

"Keep your wrist straight and strike with your knuckles, not your fingers. When you punch the bag, you want to deliver a blow that uses more than just your hand and your arm. You want to put the power of your entire body into it." He demonstrated, and the bag shook like it had been struck by a cannonball. "Now you try. Punch straight in."

She did, but the bag barely moved.

"Put your shoulder and your entire arm behind the blow," he said.

This time when she hit the bag, it swayed slightly. "I never stopped to think about it, but when you punch something, your hand hurts."

He chuckled. "Sure it does. It's not a TV show with sneaky camera angles, or one of those pro wrestling matches, where they pull their punches. In a fight, winning means hurting the bad guy more than he hurts you."

Following his instructions, she took several more swings at the punching bag.

"That's not bad for a first-timer," he said. "You've got good instincts, and you're in good shape."

"For all the good it did me when those two guys came after me," she muttered, punching the bag again.

"You kicked and hit where it hurts most, then you got away. That round was yours."

"Luck was on my side. But what if it isn't next time?" she asked, then shook her head. "I *hate* being scared."

"You're afraid because you're not sure that you'll be able to defend yourself if they came at you again. Why don't you let me teach you a few moves?"

"That would be great. Although my dad and uncle taught me a bit about guns, I don't think I could ever shoot anyone."

"If you have to point a gun, you also have to be ready to pull the trigger. If you're not, then don't pick up the weapon."

"A weapon isn't a good option for me," she admitted, "but I hate feeling helpless or totally dependent on someone else in a crisis. I need to find some method of self-defense that'll work for me." She stared at the punching bag and sighed. "If I have to depend on punching someone, I'm in trouble, too. I may get a lucky hit, but I'm no boxer."

He studied her for a moment and realized that she was right. She didn't have the upper body strength required to do real damage to an opponent who outweighed her by fifty pounds or more. "I know you've been taught a few useful hand-to-hand combat techniques, or you wouldn't have been able to break free from the pair who tried to grab you," he said, trying to come up with a strategy that would fit Drew's strength and personality.

"I know about kicking, and aiming for the eyes, nose, throat and groin. My uncle taught me those."

"Those are all good moves," Nick agreed.

"But they all require me to be facing my opponent squarely, and that's not always possible. When I'm not my facing my enemy, is there anything I can do?"

"Tell me something first. How exactly did you break their initial hold?"

"I sagged, like I was fainting, then I twisted free. They got my overcoat instead, remember?"

"Instinctive and good."

"But mostly luck."

"Okay, let's start with a few basics and move on from there. Kick off your shoes," he said, slipping out of his boots, then leading her to the mat.

She'd barely taken a step onto the soft surface when he suddenly swept her legs out from under her.

She fell down hard on her bottom, and it took her a moment to catch her breath. "You cheated! You never even gave me a chance."

"Your first lesson is to always watch your opponent."

"But you never—"

"Warned you? Bad guys cheat. You won't see it coming unless you're looking for it. Stay alert for subtle signs," he said.

Nick stepped back, waited for a second or two, then moved to sweep her legs out from under her again, but before he made contact she jumped aside.

"Good! You were looking for little clues, like my body tensing up." Before he'd even finished speaking, he hooked his leg behind hers and swept it out from under her in a lightning-fast move.

Drew fell down hard, but this time he didn't give her a chance to recover. He instantly straddled her and captured both her hands, pinning her to the mat.

In that breathless moment, she became acutely aware of everything about him. His calloused hands were strong, keeping her trapped, but gentle enough not to hurt her. As she gazed at him, her mouth dry, Nick shifted slightly, and she suddenly felt his hardness press against her center. She drew in a shaky breath.

"You're so beautiful," he said, in a jagged whisper.

For a moment she couldn't speak, all she could do was *feel*. He was all heat…and magic.

"If you'd say yes…" he murmured.

She was drowning in his gaze. Although she'd always been strong, she was losing this fight…with herself. "Stop it," she managed, her voice unsteady. "You're supposed to be teaching me how to fight."

He remained where he was a moment longer, then stood and offered her a hand up.

"Maybe this wasn't such a good idea," she said, her heart still racing.

"We're just getting started…unless you can't handle it," he added.

The unbelievable smugness in his voice was irritating. He was issuing a challenge, and she wasn't going to back down.

"I can handle you," she said, softly. Drew slowly reached for his hand, allowing him to think she had something else in mind—then swept his legs out from under him.

He crashed to the mat, rolled, and came up to face her again. "Nice move," he said, his eyes sparkling with an inner fire.

The sotto timber of his voice sang to her, awakening a side of her that had lain dormant all her life. She'd never made love, never even been truly tempted; but as she gazed into Nick's eyes, she felt a pull that was stronger than anything she'd ever known.

For a brief eternity, she remained riveted by the world she saw reflected in his eyes. Passion defined him. Then, using every shred of willpower she possessed, she tore her gaze free and stepped back, making more room between them.

Not allowing her time for second thoughts, Nick continued in his instructor's voice. "Turn around. I'm going to teach you what to do if they come at you from behind. It's a move that's guaranteed to work."

Nick wrapped his arm lightly around her in a pseudo choke hold. "The most important element is speed and surprise."

"You mean when I try to tear away?"

"No, that's precisely what you should *not* do. If you try to break free, the person holding you will just tighten his hold," he said. "I'm going to take you through this step-by-step, slowly, so you can get the idea. Think of the word s-i-n-g. First, bend your arm, and slam your elbow into your opponent's *solar plexus,* then stomp down on his *instep.* As he doubles up, make a fist and smash his *nose* like so," he said, covering her fist with his own and bringing it back toward his face. "Lastly, bring your arm down and punch his *groin,*" he said, guiding her hand downward.

As her fist brushed his groin, he drew in a sharp breath.

She sighed and instinctively leaned back into him. The hardness of his body and the gentleness of his touch were a powerful, enticing combination that whispered of forbidden pleasures and promises in the dark.

"Once the case is closed, then there'll be time for us," he whispered in her ear, then eased his hold, allowing her to turn around.

"No, Nick. There is no *us*," she said, stepping farther away from him. "Police officers and their tangled lives are part of my past, not my future."

Despite her brave words, the slow gentle smile he gave her made her tingle all the way down to her toes.

"Never say *never*. You might change your mind."

"You overestimate yourself," she said, refusing to back down. Yet, even as she spoke, temptation remained, teasing her imagination with a million what-ifs.

Chapter Eight

"So, what's the plan?" Drew asked, taking a seat.

"You'll go in ahead of me, but I'll have you covered all the way."

Nick's phone rang and he grabbed it before the second ring. He asked the caller if he could put him on speaker, then did so.

Drew heard Koval's voice clearly.

"I've gone through the surveillance video at the mall, covering the time and day Ms. Simmons reported her stalker," he said. "The feed still doesn't give us anything conclusive. I spotted a guy in a baseball cap and jacket sitting at one of the benches. While she's talking to the guard, he gets up, buys a soft drink at one of the stands, then leaves before the guard can catch up to him."

"That doesn't sound like someone making an escape," Nick said. "Were you able to make out any part of the suspect's face?"

"No. The cap he wore pretty much took care of that. All I know for sure is that he was clean shaven. I spoke to the guy at the soft drink stand, but he wasn't any help," Koval said. "Are we on schedule for tonight?"

"Yeah. We'll set out in another half hour," Nick said.

"Give me a heads up when you get here, Blacksheep."

"Copy that," he said, hanging up.

"Okay. Let's get this thing into motion," she said, standing. "Nothing like an early start."

He gazed at her for several seconds. The look was penetrating and disturbing.

"What?" she asked, at last.

"Are you really *that* uncomfortable here?"

"This is *your* turf," she said, then shrugged. "I don't belong here."

It was her tone that gave away far more than she'd realized. "And that's important to you...belonging?"

"Yeah, it is," she admitted. "You have your tribe, your clan, your beliefs, even your work as an officer on a police force—a team. All that defines you. What defines me is my love of books and my home. I can't wait to sit behind my desk at the library. That'll be the final payoff for me."

"We have something in common. We both paid a price to get where we are today, and found careers that suit us. Getting into police work was the best decision I ever made."

"You need that walk on the edge to be happy," Drew said with a nod. "I saw that same trait in my father and uncle. But I've already lived through more than my share of uncertainty. I'm planning to build a very different kind of life for myself."

"The kind someone like me can never be part of," he observed, quietly.

"We could be friends. Come by the library, once I get started there, and visit. It's a warm place filled with adventures that enrich but can't harm," she said. Then, meeting his gaze, she added, "That's the part of me I will always be able to share with you."

"But what about the private side of Drew?"

"I'll be leading an ordinary life, Nick, the kind that would bore you to tears." She took a deep breath, then let it out slowly. "But I'll sleep in peace each and every night."

"You're misjudging yourself," he said, after a long pause.

"When you had to fight, you did. Giving up never even occurred to you. And more to the point, a part of you enjoyed that challenge."

She blinked in surprise. "You don't know me very well."

"I may know you better than you know yourself."

THEY ARRIVED AT THE mall thirty-five minutes later. "Go about your usual routine and don't look for me," Nick said. "If you see a guy who, for whatever reason, reminds you of the one who was following you before, signal me by cocking your head, as if curious about something in a display."

"Got it."

Drew walked into the mall, and as usual, climbed the stairs to the second level. She walked inside Sole Brothers, her favorite shoe store and after checking out several pairs of shoes, left to go to the chain department store three businesses down. The second she turned, she saw *the guy.* He was in front of the bookstore, half-looking in her direction and closer than last time. She recognized his slouched shoulders as well as the cap and jacket. Like before, he kept his hands in his pockets as he walked.

Drew looked into the glass of the closest window display and cocked her head, signaling Nick. She didn't know where he was at the moment, but she knew he wouldn't be far.

Fighting hard to suppress the urge to run, she made her way toward the stairwell. She'd almost reached it when she felt a hand on her shoulder.

Drew jerked free and spun around, staring into the face of a man who looked surprisingly familiar.

A heartbeat later Nick came up behind the man. "Police officer," Nick growled. "Don't touch her. Step back and remove your left hand from your inside pocket—slowly."

"What the heck…"

"Do it," Nick growled.

Drew suddenly remembered where she's seen the man

before. "Nick, wait. He's my neighbor, John something. He lives in the apartment across from mine."

"My name's John Wagner," he said, as Nick cuffed and frisked him. "What's going on? Is she your girlfriend or something?"

Nick yanked a ski mask from Wagner's pocket.

Drew stared at it in surprise, as Koval rushed over to back Nick up.

"Guys, what's going on? All of a sudden it's illegal to say hello to a neighbor?" Wagner said, looking totally bewildered.

Drew found herself feeling sorry for him. Either he really didn't know what was going on, or he was an excellent actor.

Nick held up the ski mask. "Care to comment on this?"

"It's a mask for when I go skiing," he said.

"At the mall?" Koval sneered.

"No, genius, at Purgatory, Colorado. I found it beneath my car seat, so I stuck it in my pocket so I'd remember to put it back with my skis when I got back home."

"Let's go back to the station where we can have a talk," Koval said, hauling him toward the exit.

"You've got to be kidding. I haven't done anything wrong."

"If you're telling me the truth, we'll find out soon enough," Koval said. "Shut up and walk."

Drew watched them for a moment. "Do you think this is a mistake and he's got nothing to do with the other two men?" she asked Nick, as Koval disappeared from view.

"Wagner *was* following you, and there's the mask," he answered. "Let's see what kind of alibi he has to cover the times you were attacked," Nick said. "You mentioned before that he has a buddy."

"So, what do we do next?" she asked, looking around.

Several shoppers were still watching them, obviously curious about the incident.

"We return to the station. You'll need to give us your statement and clarify what you know about this neighbor of yours. Then, depending what we find out about Wagner, you might be able to go home tonight."

Even as he spoke, something inside her told her that there'd be no quick fixes. "I just don't think John's the one."

"You mean because he looks harmless or ordinary? Some of the worst criminals I've met looked like choir boys."

THEY ARRIVED AT THE STATION ten minutes later. As Nick studied the faces of his fellow officers he saw that everyone seemed to be on edge.

Leading Drew across the room to his desk, Nick pulled out a chair for her. "Wait here, I'm going to find out what's happening."

Nick had just joined a fellow detective when Chief Franklin's voice boomed out, resonating down the hall.

"Mrs. Brown, you're making a big mistake stirring this up again," he said. "We'd already made a deal with the suspect."

Nick recognized the D.A.'s name, and a second later, saw her strut down the hall toward the parking garage, a lift in her step and a hint of a smile on her lips. The chief came out into the hall next, and, seeing Nick, waved him over to his desk.

"That idiot D.A. is out to make a name for herself, so she's going to press assault charges against Ray Owens. I know that Owens has issues, but he's made some hefty contributions to our athletic league, and he also sponsors Police Casino Night for the Officer-Down Fund."

"He's still a wife beater," Nick said.

"Maybe so, but Ray had agreed to counseling, and those causes still need his support. Now Owens is back with his lawyer, claiming police harassment. Before this is over, he'll probably produce a half-dozen bought and paid for witnesses claiming he's a choir boy on the fast track for sainthood," he said, and cursed. "So listen up. I want you to steer clear of Owens and not speak to anyone about past incidents, especially lawyers, P.I.s, and the press. Of course, if D.A. Brown calls you in, you'll have to meet with her. Just watch your back."

After leaving the chief's office, Nick joined Drew back at his desk and gave her an update.

Before she could comment, Koval came up to them. "Wagner has alibis for the times Ms. Simmons was attacked—weak, but hard to disprove. He insists that he and his roommate play video games at home after work, and that's where he was both times. I'm going to find his friend, Rick Stamos, and see what he has to say, but the fact that there are two of them puts things in a different light."

"If they're our guys, they'll back up each other's alibis," Nick said.

"Yeah, that's why I did a full background check on Wagner. The guy's a weapons collector—everything from knives to firearms. I'm trying to get a warrant so I can go take a look at his collection. He hasn't lawyered up yet, so I'm going to hold him overnight. By morning, he might be willing to come clean."

"But he looked so…nice," Drew said.

"That's just one of the many tools a pervert uses to gain someone's confidence," Koval said.

"Do you need anything else from me?" Drew asked.

Koval shook his head. "I've got your statement, and our suspect's in custody."

"But that doesn't mean he wants you to leave here tonight without any protection," Nick said, giving Koval a hard look. "It's too soon for that, since the facts are still sketchy. There were also *two* men involved in the first incident, and we only have one locked up."

Koval's expression clearly said that he suspected Nick had other motives for wanting to continue protection duty, but he went along with it. "Yeah, okay. Stick with her until tomorrow, Blacksheep. Then we'll see where we're at."

As Koval strode off, Drew looked at Nick. "He thinks it's a waste of resources—you staying with me, that is."

"Do you?"

"No. I don't think John's guilty, which means there are still two men out there after me, not just one."

"Either way, you're covered. Are you ready to go?"

"To my apartment?" she asked hopefully.

Nick smiled. "Yeah. And if Koval's right, by tomorrow you'll finally be rid of me."

Drew sighed softly. A charge of excitement surrounded Nick; he was a constant temptation. Although she told herself that she didn't want a man like him in her life full time, deep down she knew she'd miss him. Being around Nick was like standing in the middle of a whirlwind. What was practical and wise could easily get lost in those strong winds.

FOLLOWING HER DIRECTIONS, Nick pulled into a large apartment complex of two-story buildings. Her residence was on the second floor, accessed up a wrought-iron stairway with side rails. The instant she opened the door and turned on the light switch, he saw why she called this place home. The decor could be summed up in two words—*soft* and *feminine*.

All the small kitchen appliances on the U-shaped counter had covers that matched the pale yellow paint on the walls. A round, glass-topped metal table, with two matching chairs, rested beneath a small chandelier. The sitting area contained two soft-cushioned, deep golden-colored easy chairs and a love seat.

On the wall opposite the seats was a cabinet filled with books of all sizes. A small TV set was placed in the open center shelf. At the end of the room opposite the kitchen was a picture window with light, flowery curtains—now closed—and a floor lamp.

White silk roses were scattered in small vases around the room. A crocheted Afghan was draped over the arm of the chair beside the lamp, and there was an embroidery hoop and basket of threads next to the other chair.

"Nice place," he said, stiffly, still holding the shotgun inside the folds of his jacket. If he'd been wearing a uniform it might have been different, but as a plainclothes officer, he figured it would be better to keep it out of sight.

As Drew glanced back at Nick, she gave him a puzzled look. "My apartment normally makes people feel welcome, even cozy, but you seem…uncomfortable."

He placed the shotgun on the counter next to a vase of white roses. "What's wrong with this picture?" he asked, with a wry smile.

"All things considered, I prefer roses to riot guns," she said, chuckling.

"Exactly. Now, if I were doing the decorating, my priorities wouldn't have been the flowers," he said, giving her a playful wink.

It had only been the most casual of flirting, yet it packed a wallop. She looked away quickly.

"I'll bring you a pillow and a comforter, and you can sleep on the couch if you'd like. Personally, I'd recommend the easy chair, with the afghan. I sit there when I'm reading late at night, and I've fallen asleep on that more times than I can count. The cushions are really soft, and if you make the chair lean back a bit, you can just melt into it."

He arched his eyebrows. "Melt?"

"Or whatever it is men do."

"I'll lean back," he answered, laughing.

He insisted on checking out the other rooms first, but he returned in seconds and gave her the all clear. Given the go-ahead, she walked over to the hall closet, and returned holding a large, fluffy comforter.

As he took it from her hands, he noticed the embroidered, lacy border.

"I know it's a little on the dainty side, but it's very warm," she said. "At my dad's house, and then my uncle's, there weren't many frilly things around. All the colors, too, were like them—forceful, strong and bold. Here, I can finally do as I please."

He nodded, understanding. "And you're enjoying that freedom."

"Very much," she answered. "So tell me. How hard is it for you and your brother to agree on the way you want things to be at your place?"

"Not hard at all. We're not into 'stuff.' Even our TV is old school, with an antenna and one of those converter boxes. We learned a long time ago to make the most out of whatever we have. Travis and I know what it's like to barely get by, so we don't need the latest whatever."

Curiosity was alive on her face, but she didn't pry. That sign of respect touched him far more than any sympathy she might have shown. That's why he chose to fill in some of the gaps. "Our dad…went his own way," Nick said, thinking just how true that was. "Then one day he just didn't come home—ever. I was fifteen and Travis thirteen."

"You must have been really scared. I was about that age when I lost my last parent."

"Travis and I had each other's backs, and that helped us cope with the situation. Travis and I had always been buds, but we became a real family back then."

"What about your mom?" she asked.

"She died when I was three. I don't even remember what she looked like, and my dad never spoke of her. He wasn't a traditionalist, worried about calling her spirit—her *chindi.*

He found his own answers in a bottle." He hardened his tone, prompting her to drop the subject.

"If you need anything, just let me know," she said, glancing over at her book bag, which she'd set down in the tiny foyer. "I'm going to do some studying, then get some sleep. Make yourself at home."

After she went into the bedroom and closed the door, he took another look around. The place was small and exuded estrogen. Then, inexplicably, he found himself smiling.

Although he'd felt like the proverbial bull in the china shop at first, there was something undeniably peaceful about her home. Nothing here threatened—except his shotgun. But that was from *his* world.

He walked over and turned out the lamp. Only a faint glow of streetlights penetrated the curtains, but after a while he could see clearly, as far as it mattered.

Time slipped by as the night wore on. Forcing himself to relax, he shifted the easy chair ninety degrees so he could keep an eye on the entrance without having to turn his head. He slept in spurts, small catnaps, the possibility of danger keeping his senses alert.

Then, close to four in the morning and half asleep, he heard a faint thump nearby.

Instantly one hundred percent awake, Nick reached for the shotgun, which was resting on the love seat. Moving silently, he went to the kitchen window and looked down into the parking lot. The glow from the muted outdoor lighting didn't reveal anyone moving about.

Then he heard the soft sound again, and this time was able to pinpoint it. Someone was coming up the metal steps. He inched back out of the kitchen and took a position behind the corner between the bedroom and bath. With his shotgun aimed at the apartment door, he crouched, waiting and listening. Footsteps stopped just outside.

Nick heard an unmistakable metallic click and low thump,

followed by the sound of metal sliding as the locking mechanism was removed. There was a small hole in the fixture now, letting in some light from outside. Using a special key, the perp had just "bumped" the lock—a skill practiced by many successful burglars and pros.

Nick thumbed off the safety on the shotgun and slipped back just a little, exposing only the barrel. Whoever was out there still had to get past the safety chain, but that would be child's play to a skilled burglar with a bolt cutter.

He glanced back at Drew's closed bedroom door. He couldn't take time to warn her. To call out now would reveal his position. As for calling backup, his cell phone was in his pocket, within reach, but talking was out of the question, and texting would force him to look away.

Braced for the worst, he kept his eye on the door and waited.

Chapter Nine

The door swung open slowly, then stopped short, as the safety chain fastened to the door and inside jamb went taut.

Nick waited, perspiration flowing down his forehead. Then, instead of seeing the jaws of a bolt cutter poking through, he found himself staring into the red laser beam of a gunsight.

The second the light flashed across his eyes, he knew he'd been seen. Nick dove to the floor just as something whacked into the wall where he'd been an instant earlier. He recognized the simultaneous thump as the discharge of a silenced weapon.

Nick fired back. The roar of the shotgun inside the apartment was deafening and the muzzle flash nearly blinded him.

Nick crouched low as he worked the slide, feeding another shell into the chamber. His ears were ringing, but so was the metal stairway. The perp was making a run for it.

Nick placed the shotgun down, grabbed his pistol, then unhooked the safety chain and reached for the door knob.

"What's going on?" Drew called, from somewhere behind him.

He saw her standing in the bedroom doorway. "Go into the bathroom, lay down in the tub, and call 911. Don't turn on any lights."

Nick pulled the door open a foot for a quick look, but

ducked back instantly as someone fired at him, this time without a silencer.

"There are two of them," he called to Drew, dropping to one knee and using the doorjamb as cover. Glancing out at an angle, he spotted movement down in the parking lot, followed by a muzzle blast from behind a carport support. Another round hit the door frame three feet to his right.

Nick dropped, rolled on his belly, then took another look from a prone position. The angle was too low, so he scrambled to his knees. As he did, he heard a car start.

"Stay inside!" he called to Drew.

As Nick raced down the stairs, a car pulled out from beneath the carport roof. Hoping to get a license number or vehicle make, he vaulted over the rail, pistol in hand. His attention on the car, he nearly collided with a man in his thirties. The ground-floor neighbor was wearing pajama bottoms, and carrying a baseball bat in one hand and cell phone in the other.

"Police officer!" Nick barked, then kept going.

By the time Nick got a good view of the exit, the vehicle had already disappeared.

He stowed his weapon, then pulled out his badge, yelling to everyone poking their heads out that he was a police officer.

Sirens soon converged outside. Seeing an unmarked cruiser come into the compound, lights flashing, Nick stepped into view, holding up his badge. The vehicle stopped right in front of him.

Nick pointed to Drew's apartment, then climbed back up the metal stairs and went inside.

"Drew!" he called out. "We gotta go."

She came out of the bedroom instantly, backpack and small suitcase in hand. "I'm ready."

Somebody knocked, and Nick turned just as Koval entered

the apartment, fumbling for the light switch. His clothing looked rumpled and he was sporting a day-old beard.

"What the hell happened here?" he asked, looking at the wooden door splintered by the shotgun blast." The station called me immediately, thinking I'd want to know, since I live a few blocks away."

"It was a hit team. The one who broke in carried a silenced pistol with a laser sight. Did Wagner make bail?" he asked.

"No. He's still in lockup. I verified that on the way over."

"So it looks like we *are* dealing with other parties," Nick said. "A second shooter gave cover fire for the one with the silencer."

"Yeah, genius, I get it," Koval growled.

Nick knew precisely what was eating Koval. Had he followed Koval's orders instead of questioning them, Drew would have been home alone—and either kidnapped or dead right now.

"We're not up against amateurs," Nick said. "Look at the time they chose, and their hardware. The whole thing was executed with care, skill and precision."

"So what are you saying, that we're dealing with military, or maybe an ex-cop with SWAT skills?" Koval asked.

"Yeah, or a mob hit team. This isn't just a stalker."

"Get her out of here, then," Koval growled. "I'll be in touch later."

Drew was ready, so Nick grabbed his shotgun and gym bag and rushed her past her neighbors to his vehicle.

They were well underway when Nick glanced over and saw her trembling. "You're okay now, Drew," he said, placing his hand over hers. Her hand was soft, like everything about her.

"That's my home, but I'll never feel safe there again."

"You're safe with me," Nick answered, his voice low. "No matter what they throw at us, they won't get past me."

"But how will you manage—with so little self-confidence?" she teased, her voice a bit steadier now.

He laughed. "I know my own capabilities, and this is what I'm trained to do."

She took a deep breath. "What I hate the most about what's happening is that sometimes I feel like the little girl I was once—at the mercy of whatever fate tosses my way."

"Like the death of your father, you mean?" he asked, gently.

"Yeah, like that," she whispered.

"I know about memories that keep replaying themselves long after the incident's passed," he answered, with a nod. "Some of the things I saw during combat still haunt me. My brother thinks that the *chindi* is responsible for wartime nightmares, but I think it's all part of being human."

Nick's vulnerability, something she hadn't seen before, drew her even more than the tough man she'd grown to know. "The *chindi*...it's like an evil ghost?"

He considered it, then shook his head. "It's more than that. It's the evil in all of us that can't join the Universal Good, so it remains earthbound. Traditionalist Navajos believe those spirits have nowhere to go, so they stick around and create problems for the living. Travis thinks that post-traumatic stress syndrome, the condition a lot of soldiers face after military combat, is all part of the problems the *chindi* create, and that an Enemy Way is needed to heal the symptoms."

"What does the ceremony do?"

"It's complicated, but basically it's meant to restore the *hózho*—the balance that allows a Navajo to walk in beauty."

A call on his cell phone interrupted them, and Nick answered, slowing the Jeep down.

"I got Koval's report. The woman's safe now?" Chief Franklin's voice came through clearly.

"Yeah. She's here with me."

"Where are you headed?"

"I haven't decided yet."

"I understand wanting to play your cards close to your chest after what happened, Blacksheep, but keep me updated."

"Roger that."

"You told him that you didn't know where we'd end up," Drew said, "but we're obviously going back to your place."

"Yeah. I'm not giving out information unless I have no other choice."

They continued down the road until they reached Nick's driveway. Nick parked and, as they got out, Crusher ran up to greet them.

Drew bent down to pet him. "I'm surprised he's so alert and excited this time of the morning—night." She gave the dog a hug and got licked in response.

As they walked down the sandy path toward the house, Crusher, who'd been leading the way, stopped and sniffed the air. Nick grabbed Drew's arm and pulled her behind him.

"Wh—?"

Nick held up his hand, signaling her to be still, and listened. There. It was nothing more than a whisper through the trees, but someone was out there in the dark.

Then Crusher began to wag his tail.

Nick muttered an oath. "Travis, you idiot, get out here before I break you in two."

Travis stepped out behind a cluster of trees. "Ease up, bro. I just got off duty and was taking a look around the area, the dog leading the way."

Drew's knees buckled, and the next thing she knew, Nick was carrying her to the house.

"I'm fine," she muttered. "Please put me down."

"Not yet."

Nick finally set her gently down on the sofa. "Are you sure you're all right?"

"Yeah, I'm sorry I passed out. I was just so relieved to see that it was just Travis—"

"*Just* me?" Travis responded.

"I meant that in a good way. For a moment, I thought all the trouble had followed us here." She forced herself to draw in a calming breath. "But we're here and alive. We should be celebrating. We deserve it." She sat up.

Travis glanced at his brother and grinned. "I like her style."

"Too bad," Nick growled. "Get out."

Travis backed out of the room, his hands up in the air.

Nick held Drew's gaze for a moment, then smiled at her slowly. "I can think of a great way for you and me to celebrate...."

If he was trying to distract her, he was doing an excellent job. A ribbon of pure heat flashed down her body, growing in intensity with each beat of her heart. "Thanks, but I've had more than I can handle tonight—today."

"You're all wound up." He stepped in front of her, so close she could feel his heat. "If you'd let me, I could do things to you that would make you forget everything—except you and me," he said, his voice deep and low.

A thrill coursed through her, but reaching down inside herself, she stepped back. "What you're offering isn't right for me. I'm not the casual sort, particularly when it comes to things that aren't...casual."

"Promises of forever don't mean much these days," he said, in a rich, low voice.

"Not from the wrong man. But coming from the right one, they make all the difference in the world. It means that love comes with commitment. I need both."

"If you change your mind, I'll be around," he said, in a neutral tone, then walked out of the room.

She sighed softly and leaned back against the cushion. The longer she was around him, the more of a temptation he became. Nick was all wrong for her. She had no doubt about that. Yet, while her mind demanded caution, everything feminine in her continued to yearn for him.

Chapter Ten

The next morning, Drew sat at the table working on her laptop, but she wasn't getting much done. "I can't stand just sitting around waiting for something to happen."

Nick's sudden grin was one of pure contentment. "I was really hoping you'd say that."

"Okay then. Where do we begin?"

"Think back to the list you made. Is there anyone there you thought was just plain bad news?"

"Rich Beck, the fire marshal," she answered, without hesitation. "As much as I respect the office he holds, the guy's a cretin."

He chuckled softly. "Rich is a real jerk, I'll give you that. He and I have had some run-ins in the past."

"What kind of run-ins?" she asked, curious.

"We were investigating a burglary where the crime had been covered up by arson, and Rich and I shared jurisdiction. He cut some corners, and that cost us the case."

Nick went to his computer across the room. "Let me do a quick background check on Beck and see what else I can get."

"What if Detective Koval discovers what we're doing?" she asked.

"He won't. Not for a while, anyway," Nick answered. "Koval's working the scene at your apartment complex. By the time he learns what we've been up to, we may be able to give him some information that'll speed the investigation along."

She waited as Nick logged into the system.

"Beck used to be a cop for the Holbrook, Arizona, PD," he said. "If he's one of the two who came after you, he's definitely got the training aspect covered."

"I'm sure he's also got friends in the PD. That could explain how he always seems to know where to find me," she said.

"But it doesn't necessarily prove that the PD has a leak, or that we have a bad cop involved. It's also possible he's completely innocent," Nick said. Then, looking at her, he added, "I say we pay him a visit and find out."

AS THEY DROVE SOUTH ON the main highway leading into Three Rivers, she glanced over at him. "I envy you," she said, softly.

He gave her a surprised look. "What's to envy?"

"You're never afraid."

"You're wrong about that," he said.

"Are you afraid now?"

"Of Beck? The guy's an idiot." He shook his head. "No, that's not it. What did you call him?" he asked, with a tiny grin.

"A cretin," she said, using the stern, authoritative tone of a stereotypical school librarian. "But here's a word of warning. With his ego, he's not going to like seeing me with you, so be on your guard."

"Just leave him to me."

As he glanced over at her, he saw that Drew was sitting on her hands, her way of keeping them steady.

Nick took a side road and pulled over to the curb. Tilting her chin up with his hand, he forced her to look at him. "Are you afraid of Beck?"

"I used to consider him a nuisance. But after all that's happened…"

Cursing himself for not having realized just how deeply the incidents had affected her, he reached for her hand and covered it with both of his. "Come on. Let's you and I take a walk. There's something we need to settle between us."

He took her down into a small canyon where a creek flowed into the La Plata River. "Some in my tribe say this spot is a place of power. I don't share my brother's Traditionalist beliefs, but I do honor them. They're part of me because I'm Navajo. So it's here, in this sacred place, that I'll make a vow to you. Your enemies are my enemies—your fight, my fight." He reached into his pocket and brought out a small leather pouch. "My brother gave this to me after we became Marines. I now give it to you to seal the vow. Inside is a bear fetish made of jet. If something should happen to me, Black Bear will still be with you and keep you under its protection always."

She brought out the small fetish. "This is a beautiful gift in every way possible," she said. "Tell me more about Bear."

"Bear is all about change and is a dependable ally in times of uncertainty."

As she looked into Nick's eyes, she felt the power that defined him. Nick was a vibrant combination of strength, courage, and the single-minded determination it took to lead a life of purpose. He was also far more complex than she'd realized. He didn't follow traditionalist ways, but he hadn't discarded those beliefs completely, either. She was starting to suspect that, although he *wanted* to be the type of man who only believed in what he could see and touch, there was another equally strong side of him that hoped there was more to life than that.

"Thank you," she said, then impulsively threw her arms around Nick and hugged him.

She'd meant it only as an expression of gratitude, but the

second his arms wrapped around her, she entered a new world—one of fire and longings too strong to resist. As she melted against him, he groaned, and the sound vibrated against her, awakening the woman within.

Nick cupped her face in his hands and lowered his mouth to hers. His kiss was gentle but insistent, coaxing and demanding at the same time. She parted her lips, offering more, and he took what she gave, his tongue mating with hers until the world spun and all she could do was cling to him. The strength of his arms and the hardness of his body filled her with a sweet, melting heat. The world ceased to exist. There was nothing but him.

At long last he eased his hold. "I'll protect you from others, but who'll protect you from me?" he whispered, darkly.

She suppressed the shiver that touched her spine, determined to pull herself together. Around him, she became someone she scarcely recognized. She'd always prized her ability to stay in control, yet, in his arms, all common sense vanished.

"Let's go," she said, refusing to look directly at him. "The men after me are about to find out I'm through running." Except maybe from herself.

"Have you ever reported Beck to anyone—maybe a supervisor?" Nick asked, as he pulled back onto the road.

"No. He's a nuisance, but he's smart enough never to say anything when other people are around. So it would have been his word against mine."

His grip tightened around the wheel. He really hoped that Beck would try to give Drew a hard time after they got there. The guy would be spitting out teeth for a week.

They arrived at Beck's home sometime later. The two-car garage door was open, bathing the driveway in light despite the late afternoon shadows. Two men were inside, working on a car.

As they got out of the Jeep, Rich Beck looked up from

beneath the hood. Seeing Drew, he grinned. "Hey, gorgeous, change your mind about hooking up?" His gaze then strayed to Nick, and he scowled. "Never mind. Guess you decided to settle for the minor leagues."

"She's with me. Show some respect," Nick snapped. His eyes shifted toward Beck's companion, who'd also looked up from his work.

Beck, a big man with a shaved head and the arms and torso of a bodybuilder, set down his wrench, then picked up a rag and began wiping grease from his hands. "Now that you've got a real close-up look at what you're missing, you going to change your mind, baby?" he said, walking out of the garage.

Nick stepped in front of Drew and casually stared at Rich.

"Let me guess," Beck said, tossing the oily rag onto the engine block. "You think that if you come across as the great protector, you'll be able to get inside her pants? I've got news for you, Blacksheep. Her legs are locked so tight she can barely walk."

"You're such a pig," Drew said.

Laughing, Beck reached around Nick to grab her, but Nick shoved the big man in the chest with the heel of his right hand. Beck staggered back and instantly threw up his fists.

"Drop him, Rich!" Beck's buddy urged.

Drew glanced around for help, but there was no one around except Beck's mechanic partner.

As Nick and Rich circled each other warily, she knew she had to put a stop to it before someone got hurt.

Spotting a garden hose coiled up by the faucet, she turned on the water full blast and aimed the spray at the interior of Beck's car.

"No, stop! That's real leather." Beck ran to the faucet and turned it off, then raced to the car. "Larry, get some towels."

"Answer two questions for us and we'll leave," Nick said. "Where were you early this morning, say four a.m., then yesterday around six p.m?"

"I don't answer to you, Blacksheep." Beck looked over at Drew. "You're wasting your time with him, sweetie. He'll give you five minutes in bed, tops, then forget all about you."

Nick took a step toward Beck, but Drew placed a hand on his arm. "Let's just go."

"Yeah, that's a real good idea," Beck said, crossing his tree-trunk arms across his chest. "You came to the wrong place for answers, Blacksheep."

Nick held his gaze, then backed away, listening for any sign of movement behind him as they returned to his Jeep. Beck wasn't above a sucker punch or two.

THEY WERE BACK ON THE road a few minutes later, driving west. "Thanks for not letting him grab me, Nick."

"You never have to take crap from anyone when I'm around."

His words resonated with conviction, and deep inside she knew she could trust him. It was her own heart that was turning traitor. If she followed her yearnings, she'd undermine everything she'd tried to do with her life. Yet, right now she would have traded nearly everything she had to lay quietly against his bare chest and allow herself to be held and protected. She sighed softly.

He heard her and smiled. "What's on your mind?"

She felt her face flush and saw him grin even wider.

Scrambling for an answer, she blurted the first thing that came to her mind. "I was just thinking of how wonderful it would be to be able to curl up in front of a fireplace with a soft afghan wrapped all around me."

"No you weren't," he said, his eyes twinkling with mischief.

"Oh, do be quiet, will you?"

THEY COULDN'T ARRIVE AT Nick's house soon enough.

"Are you hungry?" Nick asked her, going straight into the kitchen half of the big room.

"No, I'm still too wound up. How about letting me check my e-mail? That'll help me relax."

He considered it, then nodded. "Go ahead. It can't hurt. No one knows where you're at."

Reaching into her backpack, Drew pulled out her small laptop. Happy to be able to get back to at least one familiar routine, she logged on.

She soon came across one e-mail with the subject "an admirer." As she looked farther down the list, she saw that there were a total of six from the same person. Her instinct for trouble suddenly went into warp drive.

Her heart hammering a mile a minute, she took a shaky breath. "Nick, if you're not busy…"

He read her tone correctly, and came over right away.

She pointed to the screen. "I don't usually get e-mails with that header."

As she opened the first one and read the message, she gasped. There was only one sentence of text and it read:

Stop seeing the cop or you're both dead.

The rest of the e-mails detailed the many ways the sender was planning to exact his revenge because she hadn't listened to his warning.

Shaking, she leaned back and swallowed hard.

"Open his last e-mail." He glanced down at her, then added gently, "Or would you prefer I do it?"

Although there was nothing she would have liked more than to let someone else handle this, she knew she had to find the courage to face her enemy. If she didn't, she'd lose something she might never again regain—her self-respect.

"I've got it." Bracing herself, she clicked the mail open. Photos of her and Nick taken recently appeared on her screen. One showed Nick and her leaving the station, and another showed them getting out of his Jeep at her apartment building. But it was the last photo that made her heart freeze. Nick was lying prone, his severed head beside a bloodied knife.

Chapter Eleven

Drew stared wide-eyed at the photo. The caption read, "I warned you."

"Don't let him get to you." Nick placed his arm around her shoulders and pulled her to him.

"He's crazy," she whispered, trying hard not to tremble and losing the battle.

"He's messing with your mind," he said, his arm steady.

"Look at that last photo, Nick. I'm not worried about me. I'm worried about *you*," she said, sitting upright.

"He's sending pictures like that because he doesn't have what it takes to face me man-to-man. He's a coward."

She swallowed hard and tried to push her fears back so she could think clearly. "There are ways to track stuff like this."

"I'll forward these e-mails to Koval. He can pull the resources necessary to do that."

Nick reached Koval quickly and told him what they'd discovered in Drew's e-mails. "This guy's not just some caffeine-hyped computer geek with a personality disorder. His training and the way he executes a hit aren't talents you can download, like instructions for making a pipe bomb."

After he hung up, Nick glanced at Drew.

"Out of all the people you know, who do you think has the computer savvy to be able to fool around with photos like this? Someone who might also be skilled with firearms. Is it possible that you picked up your stalker on the Internet?"

"Except for the e-mails you just saw, I've never been harassed online, and that's what those guys do, at least to start with."

"Have you been able to think of anything else that might have turned you into a target?"

She stared aimlessly across the room, lost in thought. "If I'd already started working in the records department at the station, I'd worry that what's happening to me is somehow linked to that—someone who wanted something lost, erased or altered. But let's face it, if my future job at the department had anything to do with this, Beth would be the current target, and nobody's been bothering her."

Restless, she walked to the window. "So what should we do now?"

"As I said, I don't think Koval would sell anyone out, but his go-by-the-book style could be used against him. Tomorrow, I want to tail him for a while. Let's see if anyone's keeping tabs on him."

"Sounds like a good idea."

"It's getting late now," Nick said. "You're welcome to use my room to get some sleep. I'll nap out here on the sofa tonight."

She glanced down the hall, then shook her head. "I don't want to be alone right now. Let me just curl up on that big easy chair. I'll sleep there."

Nick brought a blanket from the hall closet and handed it to her. "It's heavy because it's pure wool, and it's very warm. If you're ready to go to sleep, I can dim the lights."

She shook her head again. "Don't bother. I couldn't fall asleep right now if I tried. I'll just wrap up in the blanket."

"Let me go chop some wood. The temperature has a tendency to drop fast around here, as the night wears on," he said. "I'll be out back. If you need me, call."

After hearing the door slam shut, Drew went to the window that faced the rear of the house. With the lights off, she stood to one side and watched Nick work by the glow of an old lantern. It was cold outside, but he took off his shirt jacket and, tugging up the sleeves of the dark T-shirt he wore beneath, began to work. Crusher stayed well behind him, watching and keeping Nick company.

Nick worked with rhythm and precision as he split the logs into firewood. With each powerful stroke, Drew could see his muscles flexing and stretching beneath his tight T-shirt.

Nick was as much a part of nature as the strong, stately pines that lined the limits of the lantern's glow. Everything about Nick spoke of power kept in check, and beneath that cool, controlled exterior beat the heart of a warrior who welcomed all challenges and thrived under the constant pressure they brought.

She sighed. He was far from the ideal man she'd pictured for herself. So why did she want to bury herself in his arms and welcome the fires *he'd* bring?

Seeing Nick pick up an armload of wood to carry inside, she quickly moved back to the living room.

"At least you didn't turn on the kitchen light," he said, coming in.

"Excuse me?"

"You were watching me work," he answered.

"How could you have possibly known that? I stood to the side, like you wanted—" She bit off the sentence, but by then it was too late. Seeing his grin, she exhaled softly. "You *didn't* know, not until I told you."

Although she stood halfway across the room from him, the scent of pine, juniper and musk clung to him and teased her imagination. A raw vitality enhanced everything about Nick. He was like an itch in her soul.

Part of what drew her, she was sure, was that Nick was a man of mystery. She knew so little about him. Maybe if she learned more about him, the attraction would start to fade, as it had with so many of the men she'd met since high school.

Once the wood in the big stone fireplace had caught and was burning brightly, he turned off the main light. "We might as well save on the electricity," he said, sitting on the sheepskin rug by the fire. "Come and join me for a minute or two."

He made no attempt to touch her as they sat side-by-side, staring at the flames dancing before them and listening to the cracks and occasional snaps of pine pitch.

"You seem a million miles away," she said, at last.

"I was thinking of how it used to be for Travis and me."

"Good times or bad?" she asked, softly.

Nick didn't answer right away. "Looking back now, they were neither pleasant nor unpleasant. They just…were."

He continued staring at the flames. "I remember nights in the dead of winter, when the heat from our wood stove—actually an old water heater tank we remodeled in our high school shop—was all Travis and I had to keep warm except for blankets," he said. "We made do, but we had to take turns getting up to add wood. Man, those January nights…"

"I hate being cold," she said. "I can't even imagine what you went through."

He continued gazing at the fire. "We learned all about survival the hard way. There were a lot of nights we went to bed hungry back then, but those times taught us what's really important and what isn't."

"And what's important to you now?" she asked, gently.

"My work as a detective, and restoring the order, the *hózho,*" he said.

"That's what Detective Blacksheep's all about. But what about Nick—the man? What's important to you? What makes you happy?"

"I'm satisfied with my life. It's not perfect, but I have everything I need."

"Needs and wants aren't the same thing," she insisted. "Tell me about the things you want."

His gaze seemed to go right through her. "You don't want me to answer that."

She swallowed, then forced a thin smile. "Nice dodge, but you're sidestepping my real question."

"You're better off that way." Nick stared at the flames.

"That's not why you're not answering me," she said, sensing what he'd left unsaid. "You just don't want anyone to get too close to the real you—the man behind the badge."

"Distance helps keep the proper perspective."

"Is that why you didn't want to be my bodyguard? Did you think it was too up close and personal?"

"I was working other cases," he said, then shook his head. "No, that's not the whole truth." He said nothing for several long moments. "All you really need to know is that you'll never have a better ally," he said, at last.

He'd been honest with her, and what she'd learned about Nick tonight enticed her even more. He was clearly a man whose work defined him. Yet, in his voice she'd also heard a longing for something undefinable, and the broken whispers of a wounded heart.

THEY SET OUT THE NEXT MORNING. Nick drove to the station and parked across the street from the rear entrance he knew Koval always used. Harry didn't like to use the underground garage. He hated the fumes and said they made his clothes smell. They didn't have to wait long before Koval pulled up in his sedan, parked in one of the reserved spaces, and went into the building.

"He's like a well-oiled machine," Nick said. "He'll go inside, check his messages, look through his case files, then set out again. Unless Captain Wright pulls him aside, that whole process shouldn't take him more than about twenty minutes."

Right on schedule, Koval came back out. As they wound through the early morning traffic, the route began to look familiar.

"Oh, jeez," she muttered, almost as if she'd read his mind. "I think he's going to Rich's place."

"Yeah, I think you're right."

Less than ten minutes later, they watched as Koval parked in front of Beck's house. Nick parked a distance from there, in a spot that gave him an unobstructed view. "I think Koval came here because he's been working his way down the list," Nick said.

Beck stood on the front porch with Koval and they spoke for several minutes. "Koval must have caught him on the way to work," Nick said.

More words were exchanged, then Koval turned and walked back to his vehicle.

Nick remained where he was, wanting to gauge Beck's reaction, and he wasn't disappointed. Beck stormed off to his car and jerked open the door. Still standing there, he reached into his pocket and pulled out his cell phone.

Surprised, Nick heard his own cell phone ring a moment later and answered the call.

"Blacksheep, someone from your department just paid me a visit. Was that your doing? Koval says I'm a person of interest in this business with Drew Simmons."

"You were that from the beginning, and it was your own past behavior that got you there," Nick answered.

"Detective Koval didn't mention our little meeting yesterday. Did you report it?"

"Report what?" Nick replied, in a monotone.

"Yeah, well, one good turn deserves another. I didn't give Koval my alibi because he pissed me off, but let's clear this up right now. I was at the Ute Mountain Casino both times he asked about. The casino cameras should back me up."

"I'll pass on the information," Nick said, but first he ran it by Drew.

"So that's that. But we've now lost Koval," she said.

"No, we haven't. I know exactly where he'll go next. He's at the Fresh Brew. He always stops for coffee at about this time. I think he's got a thing for one of the hostesses."

They arrived less than ten minutes later, and watched Koval come out, newspaper in one hand and a cup of coffee in the other.

"He's as predictable as a clock, and that's going to get him killed someday," Nick said.

They followed Koval, but there was nothing even remotely interesting about the detective's day. Toward the end of it, he phoned Nick and told him to come by his place.

NICK PULLED IN BEHIND Koval's car, parked in front the narrow old wooden house.

Koval ushered them inside. "You've been tailing me today," Koval said immediately. "Why?"

Drew took a look around. Everything inside the small, tastefully decorated old cottage was orderly and clean.

"I chose to be proactive," Nick responded. "*Think* about what's been happening: our location has been compromised, not once, but twice. Either I've been tailed by someone who's darned near invisible, or there's a leak in the department."

"And you thought I might be ratting you out?" Koval demanded.

Drew pushed her way between the two men. "Detective Koval, Nick was only checking to see if you'd picked up a tail you hadn't spotted yet. But all this driving around has given me an idea. Beth Michaels, the person I'm replacing, could have inadvertently opened a backdoor to the police computer network. Worried about her husband, she sometimes checks her personal accounts while she's at work. That may have made it possible for a hacker to break into the system and get into an individual officer's files. Other officers also log in from outside the station, too, and not just patrolmen running a DMV check. That could have also opened the door to an exceptional hacker."

"And from the e-mails you forwarded to me, we know we're dealing with a class-A computer geek," Koval said, with a nod. "I'll have that checked out. But don't play games with me, Blacksheep. If you have a plan, let me in on it."

"Works for me," Nick said, and gesturing to Drew, headed back out the door.

"Disaster averted," she whispered under her breath, as they stepped back outside.

"Averted?" Nick shook his head. "No. Just postponed."

Chapter Twelve

They rode in silence as they left Koval's. At long last, Nick pulled over to the side of the road leading into a campground at the edge of town.

"We need to take a closer look at how you got your job with the department."

"If you think my uncle or Beth helped me beat out the competition, you're wrong. I had to take a lot of tests and go through the entire application process. By the time we got down to the final interview, there were only two of us left."

"Who was the other person?"

"A really nice man fresh out of junior college by the name of Tim Collins. I remember him because he was very soft-spoken and had beautiful manners."

"When you got the job offer, do you know how he took the news?"

"I have no idea. I was at home when I got the call."

"How much competition was there between you two while you were waiting for those final interviews?"

"Tim wanted the job, but he wasn't pushy. He always had a smile for everyone and was a class act all the way."

"It still wouldn't hurt to take a closer look at Collins, if only to rule him out." Nick checked the Mobile Dispatch Terminal above the center console of the Jeep. As the name came up,

Nick cursed softly. "Here's something interesting. It turns out that Tim Collins is Ray Owens's stepson.

"With all the trouble Owens has been having the past few years with arrests and various run-ins with the law, he could have pushed his nephew into going after a job in records. That way, he'd have someone who could pass information on to him, or maybe alter a few facts here and there."

"Maybe. But Owens is already fighting abuse charges, so deleting a few things from the official police record wouldn't have helped him that much. The evidence in the hospital records would have still stood against him."

"Maybe Owens is involved in other things that could put him away for good."

"Like what?"

"That's what we need to find out."

"I'm still not sure I follow you. Are you thinking that Owens and Tim came after me so I wouldn't be able to take the job, and it would go to the next candidate in line?"

"It's possible Owens was afraid that you'd uncover something about him he didn't want your family to know about—your uncle in particular. Your uncle and he are business competitors."

"But what would make Owens think that I'd pass police information on to anyone? Or that my uncle Earl would accept it?"

Nick shrugged. "He may not have been willing to take the chance."

"I think you're way off the mark. Yes, my uncle Earl and Ray Owens are in the same business, but they're not in the same league. My uncle is barely getting by, running a shoe-string construction company. Ray has one of the biggest construction firms in the state."

"It's still worth looking into," Nick said.

"Owens has a lot of power, so we have to be careful. Otherwise we'll end up helping him by strengthening his claim that he's a victim of police harassment."

Nick weighed his options while running a report on Ray. "Owens is a heavy drinker who gets pulled over often late at night. The last two times, Ray was near a club called the Indigo Trail. I've never been there myself. What do you say we duck in for a quick lunch and take a look around?"

"And if we see him…?"

"It'll be an excellent chance for us to hang back and see who his drinking buddies are."

THEY ARRIVED AT THE RESTAURANT a full half hour later, parking across the street. As they passed through the restaurant's small parking lot, Nick got a surprise. "This place caters to an exclusive clientele. There are no pickups anywhere. Everything is in the luxury car category. And they changed the name of the place, too." He pointed to a sign above the discreet entrance. "It's now The Indigo Horse."

"This is definitely not the kind of place Owens would go to hire some hoods."

"No. But this is where he might go for inside information on who to hire. People in power often play dirty," Nick answered.

They walked into the foyer and were greeted by the maître d' almost instantly. "I'm sorry to inconvenience you, sir, but may I see your membership card please?"

"Is that really needed?" Nick countered, with a grin, reaching for his wallet.

"I'm afraid so, sir."

Seeing Tim and Ray Owens walking across the room following a waiter, Drew went with a spur-of-the-moment idea. "We're supposed to meet Ray Owens and his stepson, Tim, for lunch, but you're more than welcome to explain to Mr. Owens why we didn't keep our appointment," she said, then turned as if ready to leave.

"You should have told me right away that you were meeting with Mr. Owens," the maître d' said quickly. "Go right in."

Drew grabbed Nick's hand, then swept past the maitre d'. She had the strong feeling that the man was well acquainted with Owens's temper and wanted to avoid a scene.

As soon as they were inside, Nick squeezed her hand. "You're good under pressure."

"Owens and Tim are here. I saw them from the foyer. But now I can't find them."

Nick took Drew's arm and maneuvered her toward the bar. "I've got them. They're at the table near the side exit. Right now, it looks like they're having an argument."

As they sat down, Nick positioned himself so he could watch their target from the reflection in the mirror behind the bar. Owens stood and walked to the far corner of the room, cell phone to his ear.

"This place doesn't feel right to me," Drew said, slowly.

"What do you mean?" Having learned to trust her intuition a bit more, Nick glanced around the room slowly. Very few people were actually dining, and the food looked more like take-out than the kind he'd expect from a restaurant with such expensive decor.

That's when he saw three men step out from a back room. The door was attended by a burly waiter, and he controlled the flow, nodding to three other men at a table. They walked over, and the waiter let them in.

As they entered, Nick caught a glimpse of a wooden panel that blocked his view of the inner room. It was a screen, and Drew was right. The place had the smell of trouble, and not just from the tobacco that wafted through the open door. It was either a brothel or an illegal gambling operation.

Regretting having brought Drew, he looked back at Owens, who was on the move again. Instead of returning to the table where Tim waited, Owens suddenly slipped out the closest door. It was labeled a fire exit, and when opened, an alarm was supposed to go off, but none did.

Nick looked around, and to his surprise saw Travis inside the lobby, surveying the interior carefully.

For a split second their gazes met. No words had been spoken between them, but none were needed.

"Move. This place is about to be raided," Nick said, whispering the words in Drew's ear. "Head for the fire exit."

Travis, possibly having already seen Owens slipping out, moved into the area subtly, to cover the exit.

On the spur of the moment, Nick stopped by the table where Tim Collins remained sitting, bottle of beer in hand. "I'm Detective Blacksheep, Tim. No time to explain. Just come with us."

Drew gave Tim an encouraging smile.

An instant later someone yelled, "Police! This is a raid. Everyone stay where you are."

Nick hurried them out the fire exit door his brother was now guarding, "I'll explain later, bro," he said, and slipped outside, taking Tim and Drew with him.

"Jeez, man, thanks," Tim said. He then looked at Drew and smiled. "I remember you! You beat me out of that job in records."

"How are you, Tim?" she said, quietly.

At Nick's urging, they circled the block, then crossed the street to his Jeep.

"I owe you guys," Tim said. "I've applied for another position over at city hall, in their documents-and-records office, and getting caught in a raid wouldn't have looked so good on my resumé."

"You're a good person, Tim, but your stepdad's in a world of trouble," Drew said.

"Yeah? Good. I'm looking forward to the day when the police drag him out of the house and put him away for the rest of his miserable life. The way he treats my mom—he should be shot."

"So you two don't get along," Nick said, turning in his seat so he could look at Tim directly.

"Not even close. He's got a foul temper and a hard fist."

"You two get into it often?" Nick asked.

"No way, man. I'm five foot two and weigh a hundred and thirty-five. He's over six feet and has at least fifty pounds on me."

"I helped you today, Tim, so how about returning the favor?"

"What did you have in mind?"

"Have you heard about the problems Drew's been having lately?"

"Sure. Ray said that Chief Franklin's got you babysitting these days—his words, not mine."

Nick's expression grew stony. "Is that so?"

"Ray hates your guts and wants you fired. He put a lot of pressure on Chief Franklin, but Franklin has his own agenda. Getting you out of circulation was Franklin's way of compromising with Ray. My stepfather backed off because he's got other problems right now, but he'll go after you again as soon as he can."

Drew looked back down the street at the club. Officers were loading those under arrest into a white police van. Then she spotted a man standing next to a luxury sedan across the street from the club. "Isn't that Ray?"

"That's him," Tim said. "He's probably trying to figure out what happened to me. He's a dirtbag, but he always seems to have luck on his side—or maybe he just has a sixth sense. He stepped out just before everything went crazy."

Nick knew it had nothing to do with luck. Owens had received a phone call right before leaving. Something told him that Ray Owens had been tipped off about the raid, which meant he had an active source back at the station.

"If he sees me talking to you, he'll go crazy and take it out on someone, probably my mother. I better split before he sees me inside your Jeep," he said. "He knows what you drive."

"Good luck," Nick said.

"Thanks again, man." Tim slipped out of the Jeep.

"Ray got a last-minute tip from someone at the station. That's what you're thinking, too, isn't it?" Drew asked.

"Yeah, but I can't prove anything without examining cell phone records, and I can't get those without a warrant. So, for now, we're not going to say a word about this. It'll create division in the department, and I want to avoid that until I've got more to go on."

"The other officers—they're like your second family, aren't they?"

"You could say that. We understand each other because we face the same job problems and frustrations every day."

She nodded. "I remember how it was when Dad's friends from the department came over. He was a totally different person around them. He'd go into the den to play pool, and he'd joke around and laugh. Around us, he rarely said more than five words at a sitting. I spent most of my time trying to interpret his quick smiles, his glares, or worst of all, his stony silences."

"That must have been rough."

"The hardest part was that I loved him dearly and I wanted him to like being with me, too."

"His loss," Nick said, gently.

They hadn't gone more than a few blocks when Nick's cell phone rang. As he looked down at the caller ID, he grimaced. "Chief," he said, answering.

"What the heck do you think you're doing? I gave you *one* job, Detective Blacksheep, and it seems you can't even do that without screwing up."

Nick said nothing. It was better never to fill in the blanks until you knew exactly what you were up against.

"Don't give me that silent routine. Did you think you were going to get away with this?" the chief bellowed.

Nick saw Drew cringe. Chief Franklin's voice had been so loud, even she'd heard it.

"I know that for some inexplicable reason you took Ms. Simmons to The Indigo Horse," he continued. "Care to explain?"

"I hadn't been briefed that it was no longer just a restaurant. Ms. Simmons has been having a very hard time accepting our protection, so I thought a secure time-out was called for."

"You thought wrong. And the next time you get a brilliant idea like that one, check with Captain Wright or my office. You could have made a complete mess of things if you'd been detained."

"How'd you find out about this so quickly, Chief?" He suspected Ray Owens had ratted him out to his boss, and he wanted to gauge the chief's reaction.

"With half a dozen officers conducting a raid, did you really think no one would recognize you?" he slammed back. "You're walking on thin ice, Blacksheep."

The next thing he heard was a dial tone.

"Do you think it was Chief Franklin who tipped off Owens?" Drew asked him. "Once he was in the clear, Owens could have called him back to tell him, hoping to finally get you fired."

"It's too soon to come to a conclusion like that." He was about to say more when his phone rang again.

Nick identified himself and heard his brother's voice at the other end. "Heads up, bro. Don't go back to the house—at least not tonight."

"Why?" Nick asked, instantly alert. "What happened?"

"I made a quick run back there before the raid. I knew I had a long afternoon ahead of me in booking, so I went by to get my vest and check on Crusher. When I got there, I heard him barking like crazy. I grabbed the rifle and took a walk around the area. That's when I found two hikers about a quarter mile from our place armed with rifles. They said they were hunting a coyote that had killed their chickens, but they didn't look like farmers to me. I waited until they took off."

"Thanks for the warning, bro," Nick said, then hung up.

Nick pulled off to the side of the road. "We need to find a secure hideout where no one can sneak up on us."

"Another motel?"

He considered it for several long moments. "No. I have a better idea. There's a place that's not too far from here. Several agencies take turns using it as a safe house. The layout there helps make it secure. There's a driveway at the front of the house and the back's screened with coyote fencing, which is nearly impossible to scale without leaving a few body parts behind."

"How do you know it's not being used?"

"I don't. But we can drive by and check things out. You game?"

"Absolutely."

As she glanced down at the strong, scarred hands now gripping the wheel, she remembered what he'd told her about himself. Nick's confidence was more than attitude. His assurance came from having been repeatedly tested by life. Nick was a great ally because he'd never give up. The only situation Nick saw as irreversible was death.

After a long drive meant to discourage anyone who might follow them, they drove up a gravel road.

"That's it," Nick said, pointing to a house ahead.

Nick reached the end of the lane and slowed down for a look at the blue-and-white address sign on the white rail fence. Above the address were the words Welcome To, which told knowledgeable officers that the residence wasn't in use. Occupants were required to turn the sign around. The opposite side contained only the address.

"Okay, we're good to go," he said, parking toward the back, then leading her quickly up to the door.

"How are we getting inside? I would imagine that if we break in we'll set off all kinds of alarms."

"True, but I know the combination."

"And it's always the same? That doesn't sound very smart."

"It changes, but I know the formula." He gave her an exasperated look. "Is there anything you *don't* question?"

Nick keyed in the right combination, based upon the month and year, and led the way inside.

The second they entered, she scrunched up her nose. "Can we leave the door open for a bit and open up the windows? This place gives new meaning to the word stuffy."

"You can prop open the backdoor for a while. The windows can't be opened. They're all fastened shut."

She passed through the kitchen and into the living room. There was a tiny TV set on a card table, and four card table chairs scattered around. "Not exactly homey," she said.

"It's not meant to be. Wait here," he said.

She watched him check out the other rooms, including the closets. He finally returned to the living room.

"All clear," he said.

Nick never relaxed. Turning off the room light, he stood by the windows and studied the grounds.

"It's time to unwind," she said.

"Not for me." He moved to another window and studied the area outside. Several minutes later, satisfied they were safe, he joined her. She was sitting on the floor with a cup of hot tea she'd made for herself from the supplies in the kitchen.

Nick pulled out one of the chairs and straddled it. "A place this roomy would have seemed like a palace to me once," he said, his slow, steady gaze taking the room in.

"It's a nice house, but it lacks…warmth," she finished. "It needs furniture—and a woman's touch."

"I do, too," he said, then laughed when she nearly choked.

TIME PASSED, AND AS the day surrendered to the night, they found a chessboard in a hall closet and played several games. Nick and she were well matched, but Nick called it quits after they'd each won two games. "It's more balanced this way," he said.

"Balance…you've mentioned that before. That's an important part of Navajo teachings, isn't it?"

He nodded. "Navajos are taught that everything has two sides, and for there to be harmony, balance has to be achieved. Evil needs good to keep it in check, and good needs evil to remind it of its purpose. It's that way with everything—day and night, even man and woman."

"How does that apply to a man and a woman? A woman does *not* need a man to make it in the world, or vice versa."

"What I spoke about doesn't refer to an individual's ability to face life's challenges. It's meant in a more universal sense. The Navajo Way teaches that harmony requires a woman's promise and a man's strength and power. Neither can walk in beauty without the other. There's a story about First Man and First Woman that illustrates the point."

Silence stretched out as he gathered his thoughts. When he continued at long last, his voice held an almost mystical, mesmerizing quality, reminiscent of an ancient storyteller, before the time of written language.

"In the beginning, First Man and First Woman had many arguments. One day, First Woman told First Man that women could get along just fine without men. First Man assured her that men didn't need women either. So the men and women separated. Nothing went right after that, and every day things got worse. After many trials, they grew to understand that neither was complete without the other. Men and women each brought something unique to the relationship, and accepting the balance in that was part of walking in beauty."

She sighed softly. "Your tribe's culture gives you something tangible to hold on to, beliefs that can sustain you. You're lucky to be part of that."

"The Navajo Way makes sense even to those who aren't Navajo, but too many in the Anglo world dismiss it as superstition without stopping to think about the deeper meaning of the lessons."

"But where do *you* stand? I remember you once said that you're a modernist?"

"That's precisely what I am. I accept the wisdom of the old stories, but I prefer to rely on myself and deal with the here and now."

"But an outlook like that limits you, too. The best things in life can't be seen or touched—compassion, unselfishness, love. Or if you want to stick to the undeniable necessary—think of oxygen. You know you're getting enough because you're still standing there, but you can't see oxygen."

He smiled. "But if it wasn't there, my lungs would be quick to tell me. It's measurable and that's good enough for me."

Time passed slowly. The inactivity was getting to both of them, but the coffee he'd fixed for himself was finally kicking in. "I'm going to stay awake for a while longer. Why don't you try to get some sleep?"

She nodded. "That's a good idea, but I'm going to stay out here. If there's trouble, I'll know instantly and may be able to help you."

"That's not necessary."

"It is to me."

Nick watched her stretch out, folding her arm and tucking it beneath her head to use as a pillow. He remained on guard by the window, standing to one side, motionless.

Minutes ticked by. Though his focus was on the area outside, he was aware of her. She wasn't asleep. She was watching him every time he looked away.

"You'd be better off in the bed," he said, without turning around.

"It won't make any difference. My mind just won't shut down. How did you know I wasn't asleep?"

"Your breathing wasn't regular enough." But that wasn't the complete answer. Sensing her interest in him had stirred his blood. Heat coursed through his veins, hardening him, urging him to forget duty—if only for a little while.

"There are no pillows in the bed or closet, but maybe this'll help." He stripped off his jacket and, bundling it up, placed it on the floor behind her.

"Thanks, but lack of a pillow is only part of my problem. After all that's happened, I don't trust the quiet."

Her words touched a part of him he'd buried deep inside himself. He'd said much the same thing when his platoon had entered that Afghan village. Now the cries of the wounded and the dying haunted his sleep.

He took one last look outside, then turned out the hall light. "Let's hold each other for a while. Maybe we can make our own peace," he said, sitting in the far corner of the room.

She settled easily into his arms, and he felt her relax. He kissed her forehead gently. The need to protect her—not because it was his duty, but for another, deeper reason—drummed through him.

She looked up and smiled at him. Instinctively he lowered his mouth to hers, brushing her lips in a feather-light caress. He'd meant to keep it casual, but when she strained into him, a white hot, bone-melting heat jolted him to the core. Parting her mouth roughly, he tasted her, his tongue dancing and mating with hers.

She responded naturally, drinking him in, even as she

yielded to him. Blood thundered in his ears and passion drove him.

"More," she begged, softly.

As he gazed into her eyes and saw desire, dark needs coiled in his gut. Surrendering to instinct, he bent down to take her mouth again. Suddenly, light filtered through a gap in the curtains. Nick sat bolt upright as vehicle tires crunched on the graveled driveway outside.

Chapter Thirteen

Nick pulled her down to the floor, then moved to the edge of the window. Crouched to one side of the curtain, he watched the sedan drive up. The car stopped near the front door, and its headlights went out.

He hadn't switched the sign outside, not wanting to tell anyone at all that they were there. If another agency needed the house, he figured they'd either share for a few hours, or he'd have to leave. But there was no way for him to tell if the new arrival was friend or foe. The sign wasn't visible from this direction.

As he watched, the car door opened and the driver climbed out. The fact that the interior dome light hadn't come on made Nick realize their visitor was probably a professional—but professional what? Another cop wanting to use the safe house would have brought a passenger in the car, but there was no one else there.

In the moonlight, he couldn't make out any of the man's features, but when he started walking toward the house, his hand reaching beneath his jacket, readjusting something there, Nick knew they were in trouble.

As he turned to signal Drew, Nick saw that she'd already shoved her laptop and reference books into her backpack. He pointed to the backdoor, and held a finger to his lips.

Outside seconds later, he heard the sound of footsteps

drawing closer. Nick whispered to Drew, telling her to head for the car, then hugged the wall, waiting for whoever was behind them to draw closer.

"Grow up, Overtime. I saw your wheels, and you're too old to play hide-and-seek."

Nick expelled his breath in a hiss and stepped out. "Road-trip, what the heck are you doing here?"

The men stepped close and gave each other a hand slap and a fist bump. Drew, who had just reached the Jeep, stopped and watched Nick and the black man greet each other. It was clear they were friends. Considering Roadtrip was well over six feet tall and built like a water heater, that was a good thing.

"Lucky for you that you're one of the good guys. I was about to hunt you down and fill you with regret." Roadtrip looked over at Drew, who still hadn't come out into full view. "You're okay, darlin'. You're among friends." He glanced back at Nick and added, "Afraid I was going to sneak up on you and your woman?"

"Dream on. I could hear your thundering hooves the moment you stepped out of the car, you old ox." Nick turned to Drew. "This is my friend, a deputy federal marshal we call Roadtrip."

"That's a strange nickname," she said.

"He got it because he's always on the road, protecting a witness or tracking down a fugitive. He works with WITSEC. But what are you doing here, and where's your witness?"

"I pick her up the day after tomorrow. I came here ahead of schedule to check out the layout." He glanced around. "Let's go inside before the neighbors get curious."

Once they were back in the living room the men relaxed visibly. Drew noticed that Roadtrip had never asked her name or why she was with Nick. Either he already knew, or it was a form of professional courtesy between them. As she thought about it, she realized he'd never offered his real name, either.

"We'll be out of here by daybreak," Nick said.

"This place looks safe enough," he said. "Is there a problem I'm not seeing?"

"My location keeps getting compromised," Nick answered.

"A leak in the department?" he asked, eyebrows up.

"It's the answer that makes the most sense to me," Nick said. "But I can't prove it—not yet."

"I'm on my own time till tomorrow afternoon," the burly marshal said. "Why don't you let me keep watch while you catch some Z's. I can stand guard until daybreak."

Nick nodded, then looked at Drew. "If you still don't want the bed, I'm going in there," he said.

"Go ahead."

Nick walked into the empty bedroom.

"You can get some sleep, too," Roadtrip told her.

Drew shook her head and sat down in one of the chairs.

"Not yet. I've got too much adrenaline running through my system right now. I'm going to try something boring, like work. That'll make me sleepy faster than almost anything else can."

Drew sat cross-legged on the chair, while Roadtrip went to the spot by the window where Nick had stood.

After a while, she looked up and stretched. "How long have you known Nick?" she asked, unable to stem her curiosity.

"About fifteen years. My dad was a missionary on the rez and we went to the same high school."

"Was he always as driven as he is now?"

He nodded. "Yeah, and that's what kept him and his brother alive back then. He'd set a goal and follow through. They didn't have much, but they stuck it out."

"From what he's said—or left unsaid—I gather he went through his own version of hell growing up."

"That's not a time in his life he likes to talk about. I'm surprised that he mentioned it to you at all."

"He didn't say much, just a few things here and there."

"He must consider you a friend then—and with Nick, that means something. If he's your friend he'll stand by you, no matter what happens. That's what earned him the second highest honor the military gives—the DSC—Distinguished Service Cross."

"He never told me that. What happened?"

Roadtrip hesitated. "I suppose there's no harm in telling you," he said at last. "You could Google it and find out, anyway." Roadtrip went to another window, and apparently satisfied with what he saw—or didn't see—continued. "His platoon was out on what was supposed to be a routine patrol, but insurgents ambushed them. Both officers present were killed, so Nick took over. He took out a heavy machine gun that had them pinned down, then personally carried some of the wounded to safety."

"I had no idea," she said. "It explains some of his scars, the ones I can see, and the ones that aren't so easy to spot."

"War always marks you, one way or another," Roadtrip said.

She wasn't sure when she actually managed to fall asleep, but it was after daybreak when something woke her. Hearing a soft moan, she sat up and looked around quickly.

Roadtrip had moved to the kitchen window and seemed fine. Then she heard the heart-wrenching sound again, and realized it was coming from the bedroom. As she hurried into the room, the agony mirrored on Nick's face left no doubt that he was having a terrible nightmare.

As Drew approached the bed, he suddenly sat up, fully and abruptly awake.

She jumped, startled by his reaction. "Are you okay?" she managed, though her heart was beating overtime.

"Yeah. Memories…they wind themselves around my dreams," he said, rubbing the back of his neck with one hand.

"That's why I have trouble sleeping." As he got out of bed, he glanced over at her. "How about you? Did you get some rest?"

"Some," she answered. "And definitely more than your friend, Roadtrip, got. He's been at the windows all night."

"I believe it. He's one of the few people I know I can trust completely." He glanced toward the front room. "Sun's up, so we've got to get moving again."

It DIDN'T TAKE LONG FOR them to be back on the road. Faced with Nick's stony silence, she remained quiet, reasoning that he was probably trying to figure out their next move.

Suddenly realizing that she was doing exactly what she'd always done with her father and uncle—filling in the blanks when they left her out of things—she stopped herself cold.

"I don't want to play twenty questions. It's too early," she said, firmly. "What's going on?"

Nick shrugged. "I'm trying to come up with a plan. But I'm out of ideas."

"I've got a suggestion. Mayor Hensley's leaving office in a few months. Tonight he's having a going-away bash in his cabin up in the hills south of Durango, just inside the New Mexico state line. That's where he plans to retire. Since I worked in the administrative offices at city hall for a little while, and he liked the job I did, I got an invitation about a week ago."

"You're supposed to be in protective custody and you want to go to a *party?* Are you out of your mind?" he snarled.

"Think about it, Nick. First, no one knows we're going. We'll just show up. Secondly, it's only supposed to be for the staff at city hall. You'll be able to question the people I've been working with for the past few months. In a relaxed setting like that, you're bound to get insights you'd never get otherwise."

"All right—under one condition. If I pick up even a hint of trouble, we leave immediately. Agreed?"

"Deal," she answered. "But there's one problem. I can't go in wearing jeans and a sweatshirt. I'll need something a little dressier, maybe a pant suit or a long skirt and blouse."

"I can't take you shopping. Forget that." He paused, then slowly his expression changed, softening somewhat. "But there's another possibility…."

"What's that?"

"My grandmother, my *shimasáni,* lives just this side of the rez, about twenty minutes from here. She's an excellent seamstress and does work for a lot of the politicians' wives. We could go to her place and see what she's got on hand."

"That's a terrific idea," Drew said, glad for the chance to see some of Nick's roots. He was without a doubt the most fascinating man she'd ever known.

"But since my grandmother's a traditionalist, there are some ground rules you need to keep in mind," Nick said. "You already know about not using proper names. But there's more. Don't talk about illness. That's said to bring it to you. Don't talk of your plans for the following day. That's said to prevent them from coming to pass." He made a left turn off the highway. "There are lots more, so just keep your eyes on me. I'll guide you."

She nodded. "All right. Anything else?"

"Just one more thing. My grandmother is a very strong, proud woman. No matter what you see, don't feel sorry for her. She's very perceptive, and you'll put her on the defensive."

"Why do you think I'd feel sorry for her? What haven't you told me?" she pressed.

"She's got rheumatoid arthritis. Her hands are so twisted up it looks like she'd never be able to hold a needle. Yet, despite that, she's the best seamstress in the county."

"Does her disability have something to do with why you and Travis didn't move in with her when you were young?"

He nodded, turning down a narrow lane that led toward the river. "My grandfather had passed away, and she was convinced that the local authorities wouldn't find her a fit guardian. Travis and I didn't want to put it to a test."

"By staying alone, you chose the hardest road of all," she whispered.

"That was the only way my brother and I had of making sure we remained together," he answered.

"But you didn't know for sure that child services would separate you," she said, trying to understand him.

"We weren't willing to risk it, because we weren't in a position to make the final decision—the adults were."

As they reached the end of the lane, he pulled to a stop in front of a small, stucco home.

"Let's go meet her," Drew said, opening her door.

"No, wait in the car," Nick said, reaching for her arm. "We can't just walk up to the house. That would be considered extremely rude. We'll wait until she steps outside and invites us into her home. That's the traditionalist way."

A moment later a small, frail woman wearing a long, traditional Navajo skirt and a brightly colored blue velour top came out onto the porch. She waved, motioning them to approach.

As she smiled, her weathered face took on a new radiance. "My grandson doesn't usually bring his friends by," she said, ushering them into the warmth of the living room. "You must be special."

Nick nodded. "She is."

His answer surprised Drew, and for a moment she couldn't think of what to say.

"Are you hungry?" the elderly woman asked, then, looking at Nick, laughed. "Of course you are. These days, your idea of a meal is something you pick up at a window."

She led the way into the kitchen, and brought some still

warm fry bread to the table, along with a small container of honey. "Go ahead. Help yourselves."

Drew sampled the puffy, golden bread. "This is wonderful."

Nick tore off a large chunk and poured honey liberally over it. "You just made this."

Shimasání nodded and smiled, pleased with their reactions. "If I'd known you were coming, I'd have started cooking my mutton stew a few hours earlier. But tell me why you've come. You have that intense look you get when you're working to solve a difficult crime, or when something important is bothering you."

Nick swallowed more of the bread, then spoke. "My friend can't go home right now, but she needs something to wear tonight to a gathering for someone who's about to retire. Do you have something that might fit her?"

"Stand up, dear." After Drew did as she asked, the woman walked around her slowly. "Will this be for the mayor's party? I made the long skirt and blouse the mayor's wife will be wearing tonight."

Uncertain how much she could say, Drew looked at Nick. Seeing him nod, she answered. "Yes. Your grandson and I would like to attend, but I can't go in these jeans."

Shimasání studied Drew's clothes. "You're right, but I think I have something that'll fit you. I make different-size outfits for a shop in Three Rivers. Come with me," she said, then led Drew to an adjoining room and closed the door behind them.

After glancing at the array of clothing stored in the closet, *Shimasání* retrieved two items on hangers. "These represent my best work. I was going to enter them in a craft show, but you may borrow them."

Drew looked at the smooth-flowing rayon velvet blouse and crushed velvet skirt. The dark burgundy color gave them a regal air. "These are so beautiful. I couldn't possibly…"

"Yes, you can." She then looked at Drew's sneakers and laughed. "You'll also need shoes." She reached into the closet again and brought out new deerskin boots. "A friend over in Two Grey Hills made these for me. I've never worn them, but you and I seem to have about the same shoe size, so I think they'll fit you just fine."

"These things are so pretty, and you had plans for them. I'm not sure I should borrow them."

"Please, don't say no. My grandson never asks me for favors, and this is important to him or he wouldn't have brought you to me. Let me do this for him," she said, then helped Drew slip the skirt and blouse on.

"You'll need a squash blossom necklace, some earrings and a proper belt, too." *Shimasání* went to the next room and returned, holding an intricate silver concha belt with carved designs. The squash blossom necklace was crafted with green turquoise, and each blossom, like the earrings, held a dark matrix that wound like a spiderweb through each of the stones.

After *Shimasání* helped her add the finishing touches to the outfit, Drew looked in the mirror. "I feel like a fairy-tale Indian princess."

Shimasání smiled, delighted. "Now, go show yourself to my grandson."

As Drew stepped out of the room, Nick heard her and came out into the hall. For a moment he simply stared, his eyes shining with open admiration. "You look...amazing."

"You're going to need something suitable to wear as well," his grandmother said. "I have just the thing, too. I made it to thank you for some of the work you did here at the house last summer." She brought him a dark brown, hand-tailored western-style suit, then reached into a drawer and brought out a silver and turquoise bolo tie. "That was given to me in payment for a favor. It goes with the suit, and I'd like you to have it."

"*Shimasání*, thank you," he said in a low voice.

Drew saw Nick's expression soften with love as he took what she offered, never looking directly at her hands. The tender side of the fierce warrior she'd come to know touched her deeply. All the hard edges she'd seen and accepted as part of him were only one facet of this multilayered man. Love, loyalty and kindness also defined him.

THE END OF THE DAY came quickly, and Nick kissed his grandmother goodbye. "Thank you—for everything. We'll return with your things as soon as we can."

Wearing the clothes *Shimasání* had provided for both of them, they were soon underway.

As she stole a furtive look at Nick, Drew wondered about her knight in western wear. His ways were so different from hers, yet her heart welcomed the differences and the beauty of the world he'd shown her.

"She liked you," he said, interrupting her thoughts. "You never judged her or made her feel as if she were less than whole," he said, heading north down the highway.

"She's a loving, giving woman. What makes her so beautiful is the spirit that drives her, not the shape of her body."

Nick took her hand and covered it with his own.

NO MORE WORDS WERE spoken between them until sunset, when they arrived at their destination.

"Stay sharp," he warned. "Danger's close to us, no matter where we go."

Drew didn't argue. He was right. Whatever they learned tonight would come at a cost. She could feel it in her bones.

Chapter Fourteen

The mayor's cabin was nestled on a mountainside, among the trees. As they walked up they could see clearly through the wide picture windows. A roomful of people, drinks in hand, were engaged in conversation and taking in the view of the city lights far to the south.

"The crowd's larger than I expected," Nick said.

"He must have invited people from every department," Drew replied, looking toward the deck again and seeing their local D.A. "I recognize her. That's D.A. Marilyn Brown."

"I see her," he said.

As they went inside, Nick and Drew were greeted warmly.

D.A. Brown, who'd returned from the balcony, seemed most intrigued by her appearance.

"I'm surprised to see you here, Ms. Simmons," Marilyn said, softly.

"I wouldn't have missed it for the world," Drew said, noting that Nick had slipped away.

"Invited, but not expected. That was a very smart move," Marilyn said, in a whisper.

Drew greeted the mayor and his wife, then began to work the crowd. The mayor's pet, a German shepherd that prior to his retirement had been one of the county's bomb-sniffing dogs, lay in the corner, watching the gathered crowd.

Drew went over and sneaked him one of the appetizers, a pig in a blanket. The dog gulped it down, then gave her a lick. "You're welcome," she said, then giving him one last pat, moved back to mingle among the guests.

AN HOUR LATER, DREW was ready to give up. So far, she'd learned nothing that could help them. As she joined Nick once again, she shook her head, answering the unspoken question in his eyes. "And you?"

"Nothing," he said. "By and large, the people here know those in the police department only by reputation and word of mouth. Not exactly useful."

"Let's wait until the cake is cut, then we'll take off."

"You're a cake freak?" he asked, with a smile.

She laughed. "It'll be easier to slip out without gathering too much attention, if we wait till then."

A half hour later, the cake arrived. It had been made especially for the mayor by the town's best-known baker. It towered high and was filled with the intricate decorations of a culinary artist.

As two men in white uniforms carried the enormous cake into the room, the dog came over immediately and stood in their path, blocking them. There was much laughter, but the pair continued to the buffet table that had been cleared for them.

"My friends, this cake is a worthy tribute to all of you who've made my time in office so memorable," the mayor said, proudly. "Now let's share this wonderful work of art provided by Slice of Heaven Bakery," he said, then, glancing at the deliverymen, added, "This masterpiece more than makes up for the delay."

Drew noticed the dog, as he walked through the gathered crowd, then circled the table slowly, his nose sniffing the air. Finally, he sat right next to the table, staring at the cake, not moving an inch. The mayor's wife, laughing, led him away rom the table. "Jules, you naughty boy! You'll get a slice, but ou're just going to have to wait your turn."

Everyone laughed, but the dog wasn't deterred. He pushed is way to the other side of the table, then sat in line with the ake and barked and barked.

The mayor, laughing, came to drag him away, but this time, he dog wouldn't budge. "Jules, come on, boy! I know you've ot a sweet tooth, but—"

"Wait!" Nick approached the dog, then following the ani-mal's line of sight, took a closer look at the cake. "Hear that?" 'o everyone's horror, Nick pulled back his sleeve, then stuck is hand right into the middle of the bottom layer.

A gasp went around the room, but by then, it was too late. Nick twisted his hand around, then pulled it back out, dripping cing, chocolate cake, pudding of some kind, and something vrapped in what looked like duct tape. The cake sagged, and big chunk fell off the table as Nick stepped back, holding the bject in his hand. There was a faint electronic tone, getting ouder.

Drew saw the look in his eyes and knew instantly what it vas. "Bomb! Everyone get back! Down on the floor!"

Nick pushed his way through the startled guests, heading or the sliding glass door leading out onto the deck. Shoving he door open, he threw the object out as far as he could and love to the wooden deck.

There was a brilliant flash and the massive glass windows eemed to bow in, then crack and shatter into thousands of ubes. The pieces tumbled into the room just as the roar of he blast reached the crowd.

People ducked away, screaming and throwing up their arms o protect their faces as they dropped to the hard, brick floor. 'lying debris rattled around the room, then suddenly it was ery quiet. Drew turned, breaking fear's mesmeric hold, and aw Jules, the dog, lying protectively over the backs of the nayor and his wife.

"Jules knew," the mayor said, petting his dog as he and his wife stood once again. "I didn't realize he was alerting us about an explosive.

"But why would someone come after me now? My time in office is almost up!"

Drew searched the room for Nick and saw him step up onto an ottoman, wiping cake goo from his hand with a cloth napkin. "I'm a police officer. The danger's past, but everyone needs to stay here until county deputies arrive."

All cop now, Nick moved around the big room, asking questions and making a list of names, all the time reassuring the people there. As Drew watched him work, she saw the quiet intensity that marked his every move. Nick's commanding presence helped calm everyone.

After, he took the DA aside briefly, then rejoined Drew. "DA Brown will preserve the scene—the part of it that's not blown all across the rocky slope below. But you and I have to get out of here."

"I don't think it's possible that I was the target," Drew said, her voice shaking. "There just wasn't enough time for anyone to organize a hit."

"What happened lends itself to dozens of other explanations, too, I'll give you that. It's going to keep the sheriff's people busy for a while. They'll also need to question those deliverymen. But you and I have got to go *now*."

They nodded to the mayor, who was talking to DA Brown, then hurried back to the Jeep.

"Hold it," Nick said as Drew started to reach for the door handle. "Let me take a quick look before you get in." Bringing out a powerful flashlight, he gave the vehicle exterior and undercarriage a check. After he was satisfied that there were no surprises, they got in and drove off.

Drew noted the tension in his body. His eyes were focused on the road ahead and he sat ramrod straight. Nick and she had stared down danger these past few days, but this time there was something different about him. He seemed to be fighting a new enemy—himself. His brow was covered with perspiration and his breathing was uneven. The explosion... Intuition told her that the answer was tied to that. Remembering his nightmares, she wondered if his memories of combat had come crowding back into his mind.

He seemed to be waging a private battle; but as they left the mountain and got back on the main southbound road, the hard lines on his face and the grim set of his mouth softened slightly and he eased back into his seat.

Hearing his phone ring, Nick picked it up and identified himself, automatically slowing down because of the darkness outside and limited range of the headlights. "Yeah, I was there," he said, then placed the phone down and pressed Speaker so Drew could hear as well.

"Blacksheep, have you gone completely out of your mind?" Koval roared a second later. "Whatever possessed you to go to such a public gathering? Didn't you realize you'd be placing everyone else in danger?"

"It was a private party, and we gave no advance warning that we were coming."

"Things still went wrong," Koval grumbled. "What can you tell me about the bomb?"

"It was comprised of C-4, or the equivalent, wrapped in duct tape. The device was battery powered, with a blasting cap. I never saw the detonator, but I did see a timer—a cheap watch—and it had the number ten on the display. I could hear it starting to cycle down. Not knowing if we had seconds or minutes, I acted immediately and threw it out and away from everyone. It turned out to be seconds."

"Yeah, I heard."

"Someone at Slice of Heaven Bakery, or its delivery crew, must have had a hand in placing that bomb."

"We're on it. Now do *your* job and stay below the radar tonight."

"Count on it," Nick said, hanging up.

Drew glanced down at her blouse and skirt. The evening had started with an act of kindness, but death and destruction shadowed her every move these days. She shuddered.

Seeing it, Nick took her hand. "If you allow this to undermine you, and you give in to fear, you'll be giving evil even more power than it already has."

She took an unsteady breath and nodded. "You're right."

Despite his attempt to reassure her, Drew could see in the hooded eyes that gazed back at her that the incident had affected Nick as well. "When you realized we were dealing with a bomb back at the mayor's place, you did what you had to do, but for one tiny moment, as you held it in your hands, I saw something else in your eyes…."

"Don't go there," he said flatly. "What had to be done got done."

She'd wanted to bridge the gulf between them, but Nick had learned to survive by keeping his emotions at bay. Yet, what she needed now, what she'd hoped for, was the exact opposite of that.

Pulling back into herself, Drew looked out the window, watching the side of the road as the glow from the headlights probed a few feet into the darkness. Whatever separation existed between them would eventually protect her. The time would soon come for them to go separate ways. Nick needed independence as much as she needed security. It was like trying to make the north and south poles meet. Some things couldn't be done.

"I need to break the pattern," Nick said, his voice low, as if talking to himself.

"What pattern?" she asked.

"We have to go someplace off the grid—a place no one will ever find us."

"What do you have in mind?"

He considered it for several moments, then nodded. "It's

inside the reservation, and not much more than a roof and four walls. It has no running water, but there's a well," he said. His fist curled so tightly around the wheel his knuckles turned a pearly white.

Drew knew from his body language that this wasn't a decision he made easily. "So where are we going?"

"To where Travis and I grew up—a place of hardship that turned us from boys into men," he said. "Our home."

His expression was as flat as his tone of voice, yet that absence of emotion told her more than he'd ever intended. What he was about to share with her would take a toll on his soul.

Turning down the highway, they headed into the heart of Navajo country.

THE RIDE WASN'T AS LONG as it was rough. Once they left the pavement, their path became nothing more than two ruts.

"There are no signs of civilization as far as the eye can see," she said, in awe. "And the only lights around are in the sky."

"When my father built the house for my mother, they wanted a place where they could greet Sun together each morning and live in peace, away from traffic and the heartbeat of the city." There was a grim set to his mouth.

"You hate this entire area, don't you?"

"Hate is maybe too strong a word, but even though it's the safest place I know, I wouldn't have come back here for anyone else. You'll understand, once you see it."

Slowly, the vegetation changed, and a half hour later they arrived at a hogan-style house, almost hidden within a large stand of juniper trees. The entire site was surrounded by, and nearly beneath, a tall sandstone amphitheater that sheltered the building from the west, north and south.

"How long has it been since you were here?"

"I haven't returned since the day I joined the military,

though my brother visits from time to time. Squatters have avoided the place because a rumor went around that my father died here. It isn't true, but outside of family, no Navajos ever come near this place."

There was a big, dusty lock, but Nick knew where Travis had a spare key. As they stepped inside, using the light from his kerosene lantern, Drew immediately saw the toll time had taken on the interior. The canvas upholstery, on what was clearly a handmade couch, had almost disintegrated. The sheepskin rugs on the floor all showed signs of age and decay. Cobwebs hung from the ceiling beams and lined the wooden shutters. An old water heater, modified to serve as a wood and coal stove, stood in the center of the room, and vented through the ceiling by a long pipe.

Nick hesitated briefly at the doorway, then walked across the room to open the wooden-shuttered windows. The glass was dirty, but still intact.

"Stay here while I take a look around."

The two other rooms were hidden behind thick, dusty blankets, hung by wooden rods. As Nick went into each, his passage raised a small cloud into the air.

Nick soon returned to the main living area and gave her a grim smile. "No snakes. In winter, they tend to crawl in, looking for shelter. But we're definitely not going to want to use the mattresses in the bedrooms. They were homemade, but rodents have been plucking out stuffing for nesting material."

"Have you actually seen snakes in here?"

"We've always had a few living around the house. Bullsnakes, mostly."

As he went outside to gather a few things, Drew decided to take a look around. The bedroom on the left was a triangular enclosure, much like a slice of pie. Narrow at the entrance, the room was widest along the curved, outside wall. There was barely enough space for the bed, a metal-framed twin. On the wall itself, was a world map and what was left of a

Washington Redskins football poster, both held in place with thumbtacks. Hung on nails on the opposite wall were two small fishing rods with reels.

The second room was similar, but a little larger, and she knew instantly that this had been Nick's. On the outside curved wall there was a map of the Middle East, and, beside it, a Marine recruiting poster. The bed was identical to the one in the other room. On the interior walls, there was a gun rack made of deer antlers, but no rifle.

Nick came in carrying a dusty plastic gasoline can labeled "kerosene." "My brother had an old stash hidden beneath some rocks. At least we'll be able to save some battery power."

"I'm guessing this was your room?"

Nick nodded. "After my dad left, Travis kept our old room, and this one became mine. Travis did the fishing and I did the hunting. But it's a three-mile walk to the river, and the fishing's not so good around here anyway, so he'd always try to get a ride over to Big Gap reservoir. I'd hunt rabbits closer to home, so we usually had meat on the table. In the summer, we had a garden patch with melons, tomatoes and a little corn."

"It must have been really hard on both of you."

"It all worked out." He paused for several long moments. "Life for us was rough, but we were never alone. In that one way, you had it tougher than we did."

"Maybe so. Like most kids, I looked to my parents for my security. When they were gone..."

He nodded. It hadn't been the grinding poverty that had been the source of the real hardships he and his brother had faced here. Being abandoned without explanation by the one person they'd trusted instinctively was something neither of them would ever forget.

"We can't sleep in either of these rooms. It'll be too cold," he said. "We'll need the stove, which should still work. We should also get out of these clothes."

After lighting one of the rooms with the kerosene lantern,

Drew changed into her regular clothes. She folded the two-piece set Nick's grandmother had loaned her, placing the jewelry between the folds to protect it, and met Nick back at the Jeep. He was once again wearing his jeans and wool sweater.

An hour later, after gathering firewood from dried branches around the hogan, they spread a canvas ground cloth on the concrete floor in front of the stove and placed a small sleeping bag in the center. Once the fire caught, Nick went to each of the small windows and gazed out.

The light from the kerosene lamp was so low, all Drew could see of him were shadows, and the flicker of his gaze when he looked back at her.

She removed the silver-coated survival blanket she'd wrapped around her body and stood. "I have a proposition."

His eyebrows shot up.

"No, not that kind," she said, then shook her head and sighed. "Flirting comes easy to you, Nick, but you can't handle someone like me who looks beyond the moment."

There was a dangerous edge to him as he came toward her, his eyes never wavering from hers. "You think that's why I've held back, because you're too much for me?"

His steady gaze was seductive, drawing her into a world of passion and danger. Everything feminine in her yearned for a taste of the forbidden pleasures she'd find in his arms.

Nick pulled her against him, letting her feel the hardness of his body pressed intimately against her. "You want life to offer you guarantees, but it never does, sweetheart." As his embrace tightened, Nick's fingertips brushed the swell of her breast. "And desire has no rules," he whispered, his breath hot over her lips.

His body needed her, but his heart did not. If she could have had both from this man, whose capacity for love ran so deep he seldom allowed anyone to touch that side of him—that would have been worth the risk, and her heart's surrender. But as it was...

Although her body was quivering with awareness and longing, she found the strength to move away.

Nick shook his head slowly, then turned to face the fire. "When you stop being afraid to face tomorrow on its own terms, Drew, come to me. I can help you find answers to questions you've never even dared to ask."

As he walked away, she felt emptier inside than she'd ever thought possible. He was magic and chaos all rolled up into one devastating package. Taking an unsteady breath, she sat by the stove's open door and stared at the dancing fire inside. Like Nick's arms, its warmth was enticing, but within its promise of comfort lay an even greater danger.

Chapter Fifteen

Nick continued his surveillance of the area outside, checking through the front and back windows but staying out of view, and changing positions often. His pistol was still on his hip, and the shotgun was propped up against the wall, within easy reach.

"Nick, let me maintain the fire and keep watch for a while. You'll need to get at least a few hours sleep to keep your reflexes sharp."

He moved away from the window and stoked the fire. "All right. Take over."

Nick pushed the sleeping bag a bit closer to the stove and laid down.

With the exception of Nick's breathing, the silence was nearly absolute, and a bit frightening. Drew had never been anyplace where you couldn't hear some sign of civilization.

Minutes ticked by, then she heard Nick groan. The deep, anguished sound broke her heart.

"No more death, not today," he whispered. Though he seemed oblivious to it, tears stained his face as the nightmare unfolded in his mind.

The overwhelming need to console him came from the very depths of her being. Everything female in her demanded it. Drew went to his side and brushed away his tears, but he didn't wake. Seeing his features contorted by that gut-wrenching sorrow, she leaned down and kissed him gently.

He woke up instantly, and instinctively deepened the kiss, filling her mouth with his tongue, drinking her in like a dying man. "I need you. Stay," he whispered, before she could move away.

Nick's plea held a power she couldn't resist, and she melted against him.

He held her tightly and kissed her again, sending rivers of pleasure coursing through her.

When he eased his hold, she took an unsteady breath and rested her head on his shoulder. "Talk to me, Nick. What happened when you were at war?" she said, holding on to him.

He brushed a kiss on her forehead. "The truth isn't pretty," he said, his voice filled with the shadows of that darkness which shaped his dreams.

Silence stretched out, and she sensed his inner struggle. Hoping that the quiet in her would speak to the emptiness in him, she waited.

He took a long, unsteady breath. "I'm not the hero they say I am." For several long moments he said nothing else, then tightening his embrace, continued. "When I was deployed with my unit, my mission was to gather intel before our troops advanced into an unsecured area. One day, we were instructed to sweep a small mountain village in eastern Afghanistan, but our operations schedule made it impossible for me to do anything except rely on old information. I insisted that we be given another twenty-four hours, but our platoon leader refused. He said the men were up to the job, and that I should follow orders and keep my mouth shut.

"I could have gone over his head to the captain, but I didn't. We went in, essentially blind, and were ambushed. I did what I could, and eventually got the men out of there, but we paid in blood that day. Six Marines were wounded, and we lost four good men. I relive those hours every night in dream after dream. That's the price for my mistake."

"The decision wasn't yours to make, Nick, but you acted with honor when the chips were down. You did what you had to do, and risked your own life to help the others." She looked into his eyes, letting her heart speak to his. "You're a good man, Nick."

"When you look at me like that, I can almost believe it," he murmured.

The pain laced through his words called to her. His soul was reaching out to hers. He needed the warmth of unconditional love, the healing that would come from knowing he was understood and accepted just as he was.

Her heart opened instinctively. She kissed him tenderly and he responded in kind, then left a trail of kisses down the column of her throat. She sighed softly, and he growled with pure male pleasure.

"You make me crazy," he said, between breaths. Passion swept through his senses as she pulled his sweater off and kissed his bare chest, then ran her hands over him, as if trying to memorize every detail.

"Show me you want me," she whispered.

Drew's words made something inside him snap. He wound his fingers through her hair, and, pulling her head back, kissed her hard, plundering her mouth as he tugged at her clothing and swept away her undergarments. Heat pounded through him as her breasts spilled onto his hands.

"Close your eyes and just feel." He drew the tiny peaks into his mouth and suckled them. His scarred soul needed her sweetness, her innocence. His world had been too cold for too long.

Cradling his head between her hands, she pressed him to her.

He continued to love her, taking his time, and then drew back, watching the play of emotions on her face.

"More," she begged.

Seeing her eyes cloudy with desire, he stood, stripped off his jeans, then lay beside her once again. Though blood thundered through him, he told himself to hold back. Let the night last.

As he branded the soft flesh of her stomach with moist kisses, she instinctively parted her legs, granting him greater access. Her fists clenched as he caressed her in ways no one ever had.

Drew writhed and cried out his name, feeling needs as primitive as the desert night exploding inside her. As shudders wracked her body, and she came apart, Nick held her tightly against him.

"Your love makes me feel whole," he whispered, fighting to keep things slow.

Drew sighed. The warrior whose heart was encased in steel had allowed her love to reach him. There was magic in every second.

He held her against his chest for an eternity, murmuring words a man spoke only to the woman who had captured his heart.

"Teach me how to love you," she said, almost dizzy with wanting.

He was so hard, but he moved out of her reach before her hand found him. "Not yet, sweetheart. Not yet."

"Don't hold back, not anymore. Show me what you're feeling." She reached for his manhood and gently caressed him.

He sucked in his breath. "Be careful. I need you too much."

"No more words," she murmured, kissing him there.

It was unexpected, and the sudden warmth annihilated what was left of his control. He pushed her back and moved over her. Fire pulsed through him, but with his last shred of sanity, he forced himself to enter her slowly and gently. She cried out as he reached the tiny obstruction and then broke through.

"More," she pleaded.

The one word ripped through him like lightning. White-hot flames coursed through his veins. Her softness cradled him, stroking him, and creating new fires with each thrust. Pressure mounted, pounding through him. Then she angled her hips upwards, to meet his downward thrust, and cried out. Feeling her release, he followed her over that edge, losing himself in her.

TIME PASSED. WHEN HE started to shift and move away, Drew wrapped her arms even more tightly around him, holding him in place. "Not yet. Don't go."

"I'm here," he murmured.

Lifetimes passed before he finally shifted. The trace of blood on his sleeping bag was a reminder of the priceless gift she'd given him. He wanted to stay with her, to have her be a part of his life, even after the case was finished, but he knew that there were no happily ever afters for a man like him.

"Nick, is it always like that? The fire, the need, and then that feeling of…completion?" she whispered, resting against his side.

"No. That only happens when it's right."

She nuzzled into him and he tightened his hold.

THEY MADE LOVE TWO more times before daybreak. As the sun peered over the east, Nick eased his hold and moved away. It was time to get moving.

"I've never been a night person—until now," she said.

He gave her a hand up. "My brother sees dawn as the birth of a new day. To me, it was the death of night. But I'm beginning to see that the night surrenders with dignity. There are no losses, just balance."

As they both slipped into their clothes, he saw how gingerly she moved. He'd hurt her. He blasted himself for being careless and not nearly gentle enough. "I'm sorry."

"Why? What's wrong?" she asked, quickly.

"That was your first time," he managed to say, in a thick voice. "You gave me a gift I didn't deserve, and I should have been more careful—gentler—with you."

"What we shared was…perfect," she said. "I wanted your heart, not just your body, and you gave me both. That was a gift, too."

"But I have no future to share with anyone. The past owns me and will follow me until the day I die."

"It doesn't have to be that way."

"You told me that you never belonged anywhere. You want security in your life because of what came before. Can you forget all that and start with a clean slate?"

She shook her head slowly. "So we both have our own demons to battle," she answered. No promises had been made, and nothing bound them together—except the whispers of her heart.

THEY WERE ON THE MAIN road when Nick called his brother.

"You left a huge mess behind, bro," Travis said. "Manpower's stretched to the limit, and the county's asked the department to lend a hand. There's evidence all over the canyon."

"Any word on the delivery people?" Nick asked.

"The two men are regular employees who claim to have entered the bakery after closing, as usual, and picked up the cake from the bakery's walk-in. But here's the kicker. This morning the owner of the bakery discovered that the front door was unlocked—bumped by a burglar—sometime after closing."

"Sounds familiar. Does the bakery have any surveillance cameras?" Nick asked.

"Yeah. But the lenses were painted over right after a hooded figure broke in, so we've got zip. And here's more cheery news," Travis added. "Chief Franklin found out that you and Drew attended the party, and he was ready to take your badge until the mayor pointed out you were the one who saved everyone's butt."

"Did you ever backtrack the hunters around our place?"

"Yeah. And there's no way they were hunting any coyote. Their tracks led almost in a straight line from their vehicle to our home."

"Can you give me a description?"

"Not much. The closest we got to each other was around fifty yards. But if you need me…"

"I know—and thanks," Nick said, then hung up.

Drew checked her own phone for messages, then glanced over at him. "My uncle Earl left me a text message. He says he needs to talk to me as soon as possible." She tried to dial his number next, but was unable to get through. "This is very odd. I can't even get his voice mail."

They stopped for breakfast at a coffee shop, and Drew tried her uncle again.

"Nobody picks up the home phone either," she said. "Something's wrong."

"You don't *know* that."

"My intuition hasn't been wrong so far."

As they ate, Drew accessed her e-mail and tried twice to log on to her My View account, but kept getting routed to the social network's homepage. There it would ask if she wanted to sign up for the service. She went through several checks and finally realized that, somehow, her account and her My View page had been deleted.

"What's wrong?" Nick asked.

"My Web page has been deleted. Someone hacked in and unsubscribed me," she said. "I think someone's trying to get my attention."

"It seems so," he admitted, "but the two events don't have to be connected."

"But they could be, and my uncle could have become a target. Uncle Earl and I have had our differences, but he's family, and I've never known him to cry wolf."

"I could have Travis go by and check."

She shook her head. "If he says he has to see me, even though he knows the trouble I'm in, I've got to take him at his word. I have to go and make sure he's okay."

"It's my job to keep you safe. I can't agree to this."

As his phone rang, he flipped it open with one hand. "We're having breakfast and coming up with a plan of action," he said to the person on the other end.

She knew from his tone of voice that he was speaking to Travis again. Drew pointed to the coffee shop's breakfast bar and her empty napkin where her cinnamon roll had been. When Nick nodded, she took several bills out of her wallet, then pushed her purse in front of him, asking silently that he watch it for her.

As she pulled her hand back, Drew casually palmed the Jeep's keys. Nick reached for her arm, flipping the phone closed. "You were going to go on your own, weren't you?"

She sighed and nodded. "My uncle and I aren't close, but he took me in when I had nowhere else to go. Coming through for him is a matter of honor, or as your people say, 'balance.' Do you understand?"

"I understand what you're trying to do, but it's a *bad* idea." He blew out his breath in a hiss.

"You honor your debts. Why do you expect any less from me?"

"You make me crazy." He ran an exasperated hand through his hair.

"You didn't think I was so bad last night," she answered with a gentle smile.

He looked directly at her, and for one brief second, there

was nothing peaceful about the peace officer who met her gaze.

"Last night was last night," he said, in a cold voice. "Today is about survival. Focus on that."

She stared at Nick for a moment, trying to understand. The gentle lover she'd known just a few hours ago was gone, maybe forever. He was all business now, and deliberately pushing her away. Maybe he regretted what had happened between them, or thought she was making too many demands on him as a result.

"If we're going to check out your uncle, we're going to need a plan first."

"You and I will find whatever answers we need to finish what we set out to do. And don't worry about me, I am a survivor."

Chapter Sixteen

Nick parked near the rear door of what had once been a dog grooming shop. A minute later, his brother drove up in an older-model white van, with side panels that read DOWN THE DRAIN PLUMBING.

Travis climbed out and opened the back of the van as Nick and Drew left the Jeep. "I've called in some favors. Jim Quincy is a former cop who owes me. He loaned me the van and three uniforms."

They slipped the coveralls over their clothing. At Nick's insistence, Drew rode in the back.

"This is your great plan, Nick?" she muttered. "We could have just driven by slowly and taken a look. Instead, we put on these clunky disguises, and I end up hiding among the pipes and porcelain. It smells funny back here."

"The entire truck smells. Just stay out of sight until we get there," Nick said.

"I hate to point this out, but if my uncle's guarding the house and sees a van from a service he didn't call pulling up by his home, he's likely to think burglary, and go all cop on you."

"That's fine, as long as he identifies the target before he shoots," Nick said.

"Why do you think he needs to see you so badly?" Travis asked her.

"He must have found out something he needs to pass on directly to me and you, Nick."

"That possibility occurred to me, too. That's the only reason I've agreed to do this," Nick said.

They drove around the neighborhood, pretending to be looking for an address, all the time making sure they weren't being followed.

"Does he park in the garage?"

"No, the garage is filled with so much junk there's no room."

Travis parked one house up the street from Earl's home.

"Why are you parking here?" Drew asked.

"If we're being set up, they won't be able to ambush us from inside the house now. They won't have a clear line of sight. They'll have to come out to get us, and that means they'll lose the element of surprise."

Nick looked around carefully, waiting and watching before opening his door. "It looks quiet, and nothing seems out of the ordinary. Let's go take a look around."

Nick and Travis got out first, then, once she got the go-ahead, Drew stepped out, too.

"Stay behind me all the way," Nick said, then handed her a clipboard. "For show," he added, "like you're carrying the paperwork for a job estimate."

Travis reached into the back and picked up a small toolbox. Staying alert, they headed toward the front door, approaching from the garage side, so anyone looking out the front would have trouble following them. They also remained several feet apart, careful not to bunch up, as Nick led the way. Drew stayed in the middle between both men, Travis protecting their rear.

As they passed by the living room window, Nick noted the closed curtains. The house across the street was mirrored in the glass, and just beyond the porch, he suddenly saw the reflection of a man standing by a juniper, pointing a weapon at them.

"Gun!" Nick yelled, whirling around.

A rifle shot went off, shattering the window.

Nick dove toward Drew and pulled her down, using the old elm in the front yard as cover. "Stay here and keep your head down," Nick said, then rolled to his left, yanking out his pistol.

Travis, already behind cover, fired at the shooter, hitting a branch of the juniper and forcing him to duck back. Yet the tip of his rifle barrel stuck out, revealing he was still there.

"Keep this guy pinned," Nick said. "I'll cut behind you, then flank him from our left."

As Travis fired again, Nick ran toward the house across the street. The shooter held out his rifle and fired blindly twice, without exposing himself. The bullets whined overhead, way high.

Travis fired three more times, forcing the shooter to stay behind cover, as Nick hurried to the side gate, intending to slip into the backyard. After that, the suspect would be trapped between Travis and him, with nowhere to go without being shot.

Suddenly the front door of the house opened and a man in his eighties came out. "Who the heck is lighting all those firecrackers? This is October, dang it!"

The gunman fired, striking a porch post right next to the old man.

Instead of circling as he'd planned, Nick raced across the old man's lawn as Travis provided suppressing fire. About the time Nick reached the porch, the old man realized what was going on and ducked back inside.

Nick moved to the corner of the house and looked over at Travis, who nodded, his pistol aimed just ahead of his brother. Dropping low, Nick ducked and aimed around the corner.

"He's gone. He went out the back," Nick yelled to Travis.

"We almost had him," he added, as his brother hurried to join him.

"Our job is to protect and serve. You did the right thing by making the old man's safety your priority," Travis said, reloading his weapon with a fresh magazine.

Drew came out from behind cover as Nick walked back across the street to join her. "This whole thing was a setup," Nick said.

"But what about Uncle Earl and Aunt Minnie? They could be inside the house hurt—or worse!" Without waiting for an answer, Drew ran to her uncle's front porch.

Nick caught up to her before she reached the door and pulled her back. "No! Let me look things over first."

He studied the knob and lock without touching either. "Everything here looks intact," he said. "If anyone broke in, they had to have gone in through the back, or though a window."

As a vehicle roared up the block, Nick instantly pulled Drew behind cover. A heartbeat later a truck screeched to a stop and Earl Simmons jumped out.

"What's going on?" Earl demanded, looking at Nick, then at Travis, who was on the phone with dispatch. "I heard a police report about shots being fired in my neighborhood."

Nick explained why they were there and gave him the details of the shooting incident.

"I never contacted you," Earl said, as Drew came over. "In fact, I've been having some trouble with my phone. Calls aren't coming in—" He stopped abruptly and looked around, seeing the broken living room window for the first time. "Where's Minnie? Where's my wife?"

Chapter Seventeen

Earl tried to force his way past Nick, but as big as her uncle was, Nick remained in his way, as steady as Shiprock.

"Move!" Earl boomed.

"Her car's not here, so she's probably not home," Nick said in a calm voice. "Before you storm in there, we need to make sure that the people who set up the trap for Drew didn't leave any other surprises."

"If they broke into my house, they would have set off enough alarms to wake the dead. But if Minnie opened the door to an intruder—" The thought slammed into Earl hard, revitalizing his energy. "Step aside. Now!"

Drew stared at her uncle. She'd never seen him like this. The cold-blooded, calm professional she'd always known was gone. The possibility that his wife was in danger had changed him completely.

He glared at Nick. "Lead, follow or get out of my way! I need to make sure she's okay."

"If she's inside—and the door's rigged—you could kill her *and* yourself," Nick said. "We could be dealing with professionals who like to set traps."

That stopped him cold.

"I'm sure she's okay," Drew said, trying to help. "Like Nick said, her car isn't here."

Earl glared at her. "What did you do to bring this to our home?"

Shocked by his accusation, she stood there, speechless. She was trying to figure out how to answer him when a car pulled into the driveway. Seeing her aunt's old blue sedan, Drew nearly cheered.

Earl raced past all of them, and as Minnie stepped out of the car, scooped her into his arms.

It wasn't just the look on her uncle's face that touched her so deeply, it was what she saw on her aunt's face. Etched there was the utter and debilitating relief that came from realizing a loved one was safe.

"You nearly scared me to death!" Minnie said, suddenly angry. "You texted me to meet you at the bank and said it was urgent. I went right over, thinking you were in terrible trouble, but you never showed up!"

"You…got what? Text?" Earl looked at her in confusion.

"I got a text message from you, too, Uncle Earl. I tried to call you back, but I couldn't even get your voicemail," Drew said.

Minnie nodded. "That's exactly what happened to me. I couldn't get through. What's going on, Earl?"

"First, I'll need the keys to the house so my brother can check things out," Nick said, interrupting them.

Earl tossed Travis his keys but kept his arm around Minnie.

Travis jogged to the back of the house, having decided to enter through the back instead of the front, for safety reasons. His Marine Corp training in handling explosives and IEDs gave him the necessary expertise, though he didn't serve in that capacity in the Three Rivers department. As soon as he checked the interior and gave them the all clear, Nick urged them all inside.

They gathered in the living room, avoiding the shattered glass on the carpet. As Nick and Drew explained what had brought them there and into the shooter's trap, Earl's face mirrored a blend of disbelief and confusion.

"I don't know what's wrong with this idiot phone," he said, waving it around in his hand. "You all say you've been trying to call me, but I swear, this thing hasn't made a sound. And what's this about texting? If I need to speak to someone, I *talk*."

"Let me see your phone," Nick said. Earl handed it to him and Nick pressed a few of the buttons. "There are no preprogrammed telephone numbers in here," he said. "Is that the way you set it up?"

"No, I have a few in there, like my wife's cell, Drew's, the main number at the PD, and my barber's." Taking back the phone, he pressed the button on the left, and when nothing happened, tried it again. "What the—"

"What's your number?" Travis asked, and dialed as Earl recited the numbers.

Earl's phone failed to ring or even register the call.

"Are you sure that's *your* phone?" Nick asked him. "Take a closer look at it."

Earl studied it. "You're right. This one isn't mine. My phone is chipped on the side."

"Take it over to Koval. I'll call him and give him a heads-up," Nick said. "The lab boys can track it back to the original owner."

"You're thinking that someone switched my phone on purpose?"

Nick nodded. "You take it off when you're sitting in your truck. Where else, away from home, do you set it down?"

He thought about it. "At the barber's. I set it on the counter so it won't poke me in the side while I'm in the chair."

"When's the last time you were there?" Nick asked.

"Yesterday morning."

"But what about the house phone?" Minnie asked. "Drew said she tried to call home."

Nick went to the closest desk phone, picked up the receiver and listened. "Nothing. It's dead." He traced the line to the wall. "It's still plugged in."

"What about the outside? The connection leading from the street to the house box can be unplugged in a second," Travis said.

"That's probably our answer," Nick said, still on his feet. "Check that after we leave," he told Travis. "Right now, Drew and I are going to have to hit the road again. The shooter escaped, and he knows where we are."

"First, let me go talk to the officers outside. I just saw a department car pulling up across the street," Travis said. "While I'm out there, I'll also check the phone connections. Wait until I'm done, then I'll follow you till you reach the highway to make sure you don't pick up a tail."

FIVE MINUTES LATER, according to plan, Nick and Drew were on their way. Drew shifted in her seat, loosening her seat belt so she could face Nick. "It took time and trouble for the ones after me to switch my uncle's cell phone, disconnect his home phone, and even mess with my aunt's and uncle's heads like that. But I still have no idea what would make me worth all that."

"Whoever's behind it has turned this into a game," Nick answered. "He's trying to show us that he can get to you no matter what we do."

Nick picked up his phone, pressed Koval's cell number, and updated him on recent events. "Former Chief Simmons will drop off the bogus phone. Let me know what you get from it. I'm staying mobile so no one can pin us down."

Instead of an answer there was silence on the other end. Then suddenly, Nick heard Koval curse. "That maggot's on me again."

"Who?" Nick asked.

"Someone's been tailing me ever since I left the mayor's

ace up in the mountains. I've tried to turn the tables on that
n of a gun four times, but he vanishes into thin air whenever
double back on him."

"Where's he at right now?"

"He's three cars back. No, make that four. I could call a
uiser for backup, but he'd disappear the second he saw it
ming."

"Give me your twenty," Nick said, asking for Koval's
cation.

"I'm about a mile west of the Thunderbird Bar, heading
ist into town and the station," Koval said. "As soon as he
alizes where I'm going, he'll peel off on a side street and
ll lose him again. Wish we had a copter. We'd nail the punk
en."

"I'm not far from you. We can set him up."

"You've got your own assignment, so back off," Koval
apped.

"Your tail might be connected to Drew's case. If we can nail
is guy, we might be able to break this case wide open."

"Yeah, okay," he said, at last. "I'll change my destination
d head to the bank. I'll cash a check, then walk across the
reet to Petra's and order lunch."

"I'll be there in five minutes, but I need a description of
e subject's vehicle," Nick said.

"He's driving a Chevy Nova that must date back to the
venties. It's pale blue."

As Nick headed toward the downtown area, he called Travis
d updated him.

"You've got no one on your tail now, bro, except me, so
u're free and clear. You'll have plenty of backup where
u're going, so I'll have to break contact for a while. I just
t a lead on one of my cases and I need to follow through,"
avis said.

"Go for it. I've got this now."

As he hung up, Koval called. "We've caught a break. I'm

on foot now, on the way to the restaurant. The subject also left his vehicle and is about a half block behind me on the opposite side of the street. He's thin, wearing regular glasses and is carrying a laptop beneath his left arm." Koval paused. "He's taken a seat on one of the park benches and opened his computer. Probably pretending to work while he keeps watch."

"I'm less than a block from you, coming up from the south on Jefferson. I'll leave the car by the cleaners then approach on foot."

Nick picked up an old Redskin's baseball cap from the back of the SUV, then glanced at Drew. "I need you to change your appearance a bit. There's another baseball cap in the glove compartment. Take it. And how about tying your hair back in a ponytail?"

A moment later, they were walking toward the park.

As Nick's phone rang, he flipped it open with one hand.

"He's changed position. I can't see him anymore," Koval said.

"If he's really following you he'll still be close by. Head on over to Petra's. When he picks you up again, we'll spot him."

Drew looked up and down the street. "I don't see anyone who fits the description you were given. Maybe he took off."

Nick glanced around and spotted Koval heading east toward Petra's. As they turned the corner, Nick suddenly spotted a young man wearing a hooded sweatshirt and holding a pea green laptop. He was less than a hundred feet away, heading straight toward them.

Although Drew's hat concealed her face somewhat, he knew they'd both be recognized once the guy got closer. Nick quickly pulled Drew into the alley between a travel agency and yarn shop. Pressing her back to the wall, he took her mouth in a hard, searing kiss that left no possible room for objections.

As his tongue danced with hers, Nick felt her melt against him. Heat slammed into him with gale-force strength. His body tightened, and suddenly he found it difficult to remember what else was at stake.

Hearing their target scurry past them, he tore his mouth from hers and took a shuddering breath. His body was ready and aching for more, but he forced himself to step away from Drew. "I think that worked," Nick said, through clenched teeth.

"What?" she managed, her eyes still hazy, her mouth wet from his kiss.

He was fighting the temptation to kiss her again and forget everything else, when his phone rang. Suppressing a groan, he answered it.

"Nice diversion. Now it's time to close the trap," Koval said. "I'm heading into Petra's via the side entrance. Stay on him."

"This guy doesn't come across as a pro. He gets too close, for one," Nick said.

"Maybe he's a last-minute replacement," Koval said. "We can find out, once he's in custody. I'm going in now. Let's see what he does."

Nick watched Koval enter. The suspect crossed the street, hesitated for a moment, then went inside as well.

"So what now?" she asked, as Nick walked to the pedestrian crossing, waiting for the light to change.

"We're going in through the kitchen door, then catch him from behind as he tries to follow Koval back out. Stick close to me and don't interfere."

"I won't—unless you need my help."

He cursed softly. "If I need your help, I'll say so."

As they went in through the back, one of the cooks looked over from the grill. Nick nodded to him and held up his badge, and the man went back to his work. A moment later, they entered the dining area and saw Koval paying for his carry-out at the cash register. Their suspect had seated himself at a bench just inside the door and had his laptop open again. When Koval went out the front door he closed the laptop and followed.

Nick intended to cut him off at the door, but the man suddenly spotted Nick closing in and ran outside, racing down the sidewalk and dodging people in his way. Nick was on his heels, Drew right beside him.

"Stop! Police officer," Nick yelled.

Seeing that Nick was catching up, the man suddenly hurled the laptop out into the middle of the street. Drew knew that as soon as the light turned, and traffic got underway again, whatever information the laptop contained would be destroyed, if it wasn't already. Holding her hand up high over her head, signaling drivers to remain at a stop, she darted out into traffic. The light turned green but the cars remained in place, though horns blared and angry drivers yelled out curses.

Drew scooped up the laptop and raced toward the sidewalk. As a motorcycle came rushing around the corner, she heard the squeal of tires inches from her. Drew jumped the last few feet to the curb, her heart in her throat.

Hands shaking, and gasping for breath, Drew looked down at the computer and smiled. It was a sturdy machine, and though scratched and scraped, there was no major damage that she could see.

Hearing footsteps closing in, Drew turned and saw Nick running up, his wrist attached to his handcuffed prisoner's.

Onlookers had stopped, curious what was going on, but as Nick joined her with his prisoner, people stepped back, giving them lots of room.

"Are you out of your mind?" Nick yelled. "Don't ever do something that crazy again!"

"I'm fine. Relax. I figured that he tossed the computer into the street, hoping it would get run over. Then he wouldn't have to explain whatever was on the hard drive. Now that it's safe, we can find out what is so secret."

As she got a close look at Nick's prisoner, Drew realized that he was more boy than man. He was seventeen at most—maybe even sixteen.

"I'm telling you. You got the wrong guy. I don't know nuthin'," the kid muttered.

Nick tightened his grip on the boy's arm. "You're in a world of trouble, kid. Holding out on us now isn't going to do you much good," he said.

"You've got me confused with someone else, dude."

"Where's Koval?" Drew asked, looking around.

"He helped me corral the kid, then went back for his vehicle. He should be here in five." Nick stared into the boy's face, but the kid wouldn't make eye contact. From the way he'd tried to get rid of the laptop, Nick knew he was guilty of something, maybe theft. But whether he had anything at all to do with Drew's case remained to be seen.

Nick quickly mirandized the young man. "If you cooperate with us and answer our questions truthfully, I guarantee the district attorney will cut you some slack. That's your best chance right now," Nick said.

"Does that mean I won't be arrested?" the kid asked, quickly.

"I can't just let you walk away. But if you cooperate with our investigation you should be out of jail in a few hours."

The kid shook his head. "No deal. Promise to let me go, and I'll tell you whatever you want."

"I can't guarantee anything until I know just how deep you're in, kid. If you're involved in kidnaping or attempted murder, there may not be much I can do to help you."

The boy's face went as white as a sheet. "I had nothing to do with anything like that. I swear. All I've done is a little computer work—hacking into a few accounts, stuff like that."

"If what you're saying is true, you'll probably get off with nothing more than probation. But you've got to talk to me now."

"What do you want to know?" he asked.

"You're not carrying any ID, so start with your name."

"Marc Lassen."

"How old are you, son?"

"Almost seventeen."

"Who hired you to tail Detective Koval?"

"I don't know. I was hired over the Internet—Lazlowslist. Initially, all I was paid to do was hack into Drew Simmons's e-mail."

"Why?" she asked.

"The guy who hired me said you'd dumped him and he wanted to get back at you." Marc cocked his head toward the laptop Drew had rescued. "My password is Hal2001Dave. Check it out. If it'll still boot up, you'll see. His e-mails are all in there. His screen name's Persecutor. I figured that he's really into gaming."

"Or maybe he's just a sicko," Drew muttered, under her breath.

"What else can you tell me?" Nick asked Marc.

"The guy told me to come up with some seriously terrifying e-mails. That's why I decided to have a little fun enhancing the photos. Persecutor said he wanted you to suffer. That's exactly the way he said it, too. Go into e-mail, you'll see."

Drew looked it up, and a moment later nodded. "It's all in here," she told Nick, then looked at Marc. "Didn't you ever wonder who the man was?"

"Yeah, of course. I tried to hack into his e-mail account, but he never used the same URL or IP address twice. There are sites that deliberately hide your identity, so I figured that was why I never got anywhere."

"How did you get paid?" Nick asked.

"I got some crazy apps, man, the kind I would never have

been able to afford on my own. And I got that laptop, too. It's a civilian, heavy-duty version of the ones the army uses. That's why it probably survived me tossing it out in the street. I found it out on my doorstep one morning. Can you believe it? That one's *the* top of the line."

"It's also stolen," Drew said. "I just checked the user accounts set up when the computer was first purchased. There's someone else's name and photograph there. There are also several Internet service provider accounts on this thing. One of them is set up under the name James Wright. Isn't that Captain Wright?" she asked Nick.

"It's a common name, but it does raise some interesting questions. Maybe he's been targeted and hasn't said anything, for his own reasons," Nick said. "Did you put it there, Marc?"

"Nah. Those were all there when I got it."

Seeing Koval parking across the street, Nick called Drew's attention to the car. "Come on. Let's go."

Drew closed up the computer and fell into step beside Nick and Marc as they crossed the street.

"Koval's not going to like the fact that I've already questioned Marc. Be prepared for a minor explosion," he warned Drew.

"But you'll back me up, right?" Marc asked. "I've cooperated, so that means I'll stay out of jail."

"You'll make probation, and there's a good chance that the charges will be reduced to some slap-on-the-wrist time," Nick said. "But you'll have to answer more questions."

Koval was waiting for them on the sidewalk and took custody of the boy. As Nick briefed him, Koval's expression grew hostile. "You should have waited to question my suspect until I was present. This is my case and—"

"Hey, it's done and you'll get the collar. We'll get things sorted out later."

As Koval opened the door to the backseat, ready to secure

their prisoner, a sedan cruising down the street suddenly accelerated toward them. A man holding a pistol leaned out the passenger's side window and began firing.

Chapter Eighteen

Marc's body shook from the impact of multiple strikes, even as Koval pushed him down behind the vehicle. As the gunman fired again, Koval took a hit to the chest and staggered back.

Nick grabbed Drew, threw her down to the sidewalk and reached for his weapon. The sedan raced away, but Nick ran after it and snapped off three quick shots. Although he shattered the back window, the car kept going. It swerved around a corner, racing past bystanders on sidewalks and forcing Nick to hold his fire.

Cursing, he took a look around him. The street had quickly become a mass of confusion. Yelling for someone to call 911, Nick raced back to Drew and Koval. Drew was next to Marc, who now lay crumpled against the side of Koval's unit, his chest soaked with blood.

Koval was sitting up, groaning in agony, but there was no blood on his chest. "Vest," he muttered, answering Nick's unspoken question. "Feels like...kicked by a horse."

"We need a doctor!" Drew cried out, horrified by the expanding pool of blood around the boy.

"It's too late for him," Nick said, as he looked into Marc's vacant eyes. He checked the pulse point at Marc's neck, mostly to comply with training, but he knew death when he saw it.

Nick called in the incident and a description of the car.

"They didn't come for you two. They wanted the kid. I just got in the way," Koval said, after Nick hung up. "Did either of you get a good look at the shooter?"

Drew shook her head, still swallowing hard. "It happened too fast."

"I got a flash—black baseball cap over dark brown hair, skin lighter than mine, clean shaven, sunglasses. But I didn't recognize him," Nick said.

"Any chance you could ID him?" Koval asked.

"Probably not. What I got was an overall impression, and the .45 auto was an M-1911, or a clone. He wasn't wearing gloves, so if we find the car…"

"We may get prints," Koval said, finishing for him. "You better take Drew to the station. She'll be safer there."

"Yeah. Even if one our own is involved, he won't go after her there," Nick said, with a nod.

"Get going. I'll secure the scene," Koval said.

WHEN NICK AND DREW arrived at the station, Captain Wright was there to meet them. "In here, detective," he said. "You, too, young lady."

They followed him into the office.

"I'm glad to see you're both okay," Captain Wright said, closing the door behind them.

Aware that the captain's name had appeared on the computer she held in her arms, Drew glanced at Nick and waited.

Nick made his incident report, beginning with the ambush at the Simmons's residence, and ending with Marc Lassen's murder. "The laptop Drew is holding was in Lassen's possession and promises to hold the most evidence. We've already found some interesting names on it—yours, for one."

Wright's face grew stony, his eyes cold and lethal. "What exactly are you implying?"

"I'm just stating a fact," Nick answered. "Before he died,

Lassen stated that the account with your name had already been stored on the hard drive when he got the computer. We also found the name of the original owner in the setup files, so the techs should be able to contact him."

Hearing the door open, they glanced back and saw Chief Franklin come in and Captain Wright briefed him.

Chief Franklin looked at the computer Drew still held.

"That'll have to go down to the lab," he said, then went to the door and called one of the officers. A stern-looking sergeant took it from Drew, then had her and Nick sign the evidence log, so the chain of custody could be preserved.

"Chief, I have no idea what my name's doing on that thing," Captain Wright said. "One of my credit cards was compromised when the online site of a merchant I deal with frequently got hacked. I reported it, and also destroyed the card. That was the end of it as far as I was concerned—till now."

"In all fairness, it wouldn't be that difficult for someone who's computer savvy to fake an account," Drew said. "And our names are on it as well. We're the victims, so the fact that your name's there, Captain, isn't indicative of anything in particular."

Captain Wright gave her a grateful smile.

"You said you questioned Lassen before he died," Chief Franklin said, looking at Nick.

Nick nodded. "He was just a kid who got in over his head, trying to make some quick scores. I don't think he was lying when he told me he didn't know who hired him."

There was a knock on the door, and one of the men from the crime lab came in. "We were able to download the hard drive. According to the manufacturer, the original owner was a geologist who works at a mining operation in southern New Mexico. He reported the laptop stolen about a month ago. I thought you all might want to come down and take a look at the other information we found on it."

"Let's go," Chief Franklin answered, then addressed Drew. "You'll have to wait for us here."

Drew left the office, and as she walked down the hall to the vending machine, spotted Travis. He saw her, and with a smile, came over. "Looks like you can use some company."

"Your brother's at the lab with the chief. I wasn't invited to go with them." Drew blew out a long breath. "I hate taking orders—*stay, come, go.* Ugh!"

He took her into the break room. "We all answer to someone—it's part of life."

"Nick's older than you. Did he order you around when you were kids?"

Travis chuckled. "He tried, but I usually had my own ideas."

"That must have made things difficult. I've noticed your brother likes to be in charge," she said, sourly.

"Sure he does, but a little adversity molds character, and I like to think I've done my part," he said, then, with a gleam in his eyes added, "My brother really does need someone like you, who stands up to him. That's the only way he'll ever achieve balance and walk in beauty."

"But I understand he doesn't follow Navajo ways."

"Navajo ways require more from him than he can give right now. My brother has a lot of anger inside him. Some of it is focused on our father, and is tied to the things we were forced to do to survive. Then there's the Afghan battle and the toll it took on his unit. Many ghosts haunt him."

"We all have to come to terms with our past," she said, in a whisper-soft voice.

Before Travis could answer, Nick appeared in the doorway. "Let's go," he said, looking at Drew. "Time for us to get moving." He glanced at his brother. "I've been second-guessed a lot lately. Double-check your phone for bugs—and keep watching your tail."

"Consider it done. But the same goes for you," Travis said.

"I'll be taking my phone apart, and hers, too, just as soon as we're clear of the station. But I need a favor, bro. When's the last time you checked your vehicle for bugs?"

"Earlier this morning. I was going to talk to a source I need to protect, so I swept it from top to bottom," Travis said. "Well, I did a visual, then had a tech do an electronic sweep out in the garage."

"Smart. How about switching your wheels with mine?"

"That's a good idea," Travis said, tossing his brother the keys. "I can also have your Jeep swept. My pickup's parked just around the corner, right next to the construction site—"

"And the video store," Nick said, finishing for him. "You've been parking there a lot lately. Are you dating one of the clerks, or do you all of a sudden have a thing for videos?" Nick asked, with a half grin.

"I like to browse," Travis said.

Nick laughed and walked quickly out into the parking garage with Drew. The side exit from this part of the station would put them closer to Travis's truck.

Nick glanced at the construction site across the street, where the steel frame of an office building was now up to four stories. A large crane was positioned on the street, and suspended beneath it, on heavy cables, rested a large metal beam that had apparently just been lifted off a tractor trailer. The place was quiet now, so he surmised the crew was on lunch break.

As they approached Travis's pickup, they heard the crane start up. The arm of the crane carrying the beam swung out into the street with a jerky motion that set the load swaying back and forth.

Nick stopped. "Whoa, that crane operator had better take it easy. That load's not stable."

"Maybe he had a few beers for lunch."

Nick grabbed Drew's arm. "Stay back, he's losing control," he said, as the crane arm moved forward, its load descending erratically.

"Hey!" Nick yelled. He turned his back on the suspended load for a second and stepped away, waving and trying to position himself so the operator could see him.

As Drew looked back toward the beam, the cable holding it suddenly come loose and the steel girder fell out of the loops like a two-ton missile.

"Nick!" Drew crashed into Nick from behind, pushing him out of the way. They collided with a stack of metal tubing, part of a dismantled scaffold, and they fell to the pavement as the ground shook like an earthquake.

Nick twisted around and pulled Drew beneath him. Dust flew everywhere, and an ear-shattering clang rose in the air, as sections of scaffold bounced, trapping them behind a cage of steel.

Rising slowly to their knees, they saw the massive steel beam on the pavement. It had hit at an angle, peeling back a chunk of the asphalt. Tangled in cables as big around as her wrist, the crane's load had missed Travis's pickup by a mere ten feet.

"That crane operator just tried to kill us," Nick spat out, grabbing a section of scaffolding and pushing it away. The metal tubes crashed to the pavement, freeing them from their temporary prison.

Nick scrambled out, looking up at the crane. The operator was gone, though the machine was still running.

"Call Koval and tell him what happened," Nick said, in an unsteady voice, as people rushed out of the neighboring shops and the police garage across the street.

"You're hurt!" she said, her voice two octaves higher than normal, as she saw him rubbing his side and fighting to catch his breath. "Do you need to go to a hospital?"

He shook his head. "Got poked in the ribs with a piece of

pipe, but the vest protected me. Help me to Travis's truck. We need to get out of here," he said, giving the closest officer a thumbs up, signaling he was okay.

"You're *not* okay and you're *not* driving. You can't even breathe," Drew said, taking the keys from Nick. "Once you catch your breath, *you* make the phone call to Koval. I'll take the wheel." As she switched on the ignition, the engine roared to life. "What does he have under the hood of this monster—a nuclear reactor?"

"Hemi engine, heavy duty suspension, chromed chrome— the works." He tried to even his breathing. "He could probably tow my Jeep faster than it'll go on its own. Cost about three times as much, though. Drive faster. I'll check for a tail," Nick said, his voice a little steadier now, as he punched numbers on his cell phone.

"Are you sure you don't need a hospital?" she asked.

"Yes. I'll have a bruise. That's all," he said. "But you and I need to talk. What you did—"

Koval picked up on the other end just then, and Nick briefed him in a short, staccato burst. After a few moments, he flipped the phone shut.

"What did Koval say?" she asked.

"They'll process the crane and see if they can find out who was at the controls," he said. "Fortunately, no one took a direct hit and nothing was really damaged, except for that big divot in the road. But what the hell were you thinking, running right into danger like that?"

"Later," she answered, calmly. "Right now I need to know where we're going. If I stay on this street, we'll be out of town in five minutes. Do you want me to keep heading northeast?"

Nick nodded and straightened in his seat. "I'm going to call my brother. But first things first." He took the phone apart, and after making sure there were no bugs or tracking devices hidden within, dialed.

Travis answered on the first ring. "I'm glad to hear you're okay," he said. "Now what about my truck?"

After assuring Travis that his pickup hadn't been damaged, Nick gave him a rundown. "Someone's selling us out," Nick said.

"Any idea who or how?"

"Not yet, but I have a plan," Nick said.

"Put your brother on the speaker," Drew said, interrupting him. "I'm part of this, too."

Knowing he'd never know a moment's peace unless he complied, Nick did as she asked, and placed the phone on the console between them.

"Here's my idea," Nick began. "Tell Wright that you spoke to me and I'm heading to the Painted Dove motel on the eastern edge of town. Then tell the chief the same thing, except for the location. Say I changed my mind at the last minute, and we're headed to one of the cabins at the River Walk Campgrounds. Then you can watch one place, and Koval the other. That'll tell us once and for all if either of those men are passing on information."

"Good plan," Drew whispered.

"In the meantime, bro, I'll have to find a good safe house for real. I'm going to need a breather. I ran into some scaffolding and it knocked the wind out of me."

"You sure you're okay?" Travis asked.

"Yeah, just racked up a little. But I'd like an hour or so to regroup."

"Here's a thought. Remember the time we hid out from social services? We went to a place no one would find us."

"That's a great idea," Nick said.

"Hopefully, I'll have some information for you later. I'll be in touch."

Nick put the phone away and gave Drew directions. "It's a secluded cabin near Todosio Canyon, north of the lake. It should take us a little over an hour to get there."

She saw Nick lean back, still favoring his side, and knew he was hurting far more than he'd admit. Knowing that a little down time was all the help he'd accept, she said, "Get some rest. I'll let you know when we reach the turnoff."

Chapter Nineteen

They arrived at a cabin overlooking the western channel of Navajo Lake, Los Pinos River, a half hour later.

"This is it," Nick said, pointing to the narrow structure ahead, beneath a pine tree.

As Nick walked up the rocky path, she watched him closely. He seemed steadier on his feet now. "I was really worried about you for a while, Nick. I thought you were purposely playing things down, and giving me the macho version of the story."

"The vest protected me, but I'm still sore."

He found the key at the usual spot and led the way inside. The place looked as if it hadn't been used since summer.

As he pulled the cover off the couch with one sweeping motion, he sucked in a ragged breath.

Hearing it, she realized that he was worse off than he'd led her to believe and hurried to his side. "Let me make sure you don't have a broken rib or two. I know what to look for. My ex-roommate was a med student," she said. "Take off your jacket and vest so I can look you over."

"You can look me over anytime," he said, but as he moved to slip out of his jacket, he winced.

"Let me help you," she said, gently.

Bare chested, he sat as she ran her fingertips over the angry deep red bruise on his side. "Keep this up, woman, and you're going to get more of a response than you were expecting."

She refused to take the bait. "You took quite a jab, but there's no sign of a break."

"As I told you, I'll be black-and-blue for a while, but I'll live. Satisfied?"

She nodded. Nick was magnificent—all hard ridges and planes, and just the sight of him made her heart beat faster. She sighed softly, and as she looked up, saw that his gaze was focused on her. The intensity she saw in his eyes made a shiver course up her spine. She took a step back, but before she could take another, Nick pulled her into his arms and took her mouth in a deep and possessive kiss that shook her to the core.

His body was hard and hot, and she held on to him, her head spinning with emotions. He was all passion and fire, and she gave herself to him, welcoming all his demands.

Tearing his mouth from hers a lifetime later, he took a breath and cursed. "You make me crazy," he growled. "But, woman, if you ever pull another stunt like the one you did today, I'll shoot you myself. Do you hear me? It's *my* job to keep you safe, not vice versa. You deliberately ran in the path of that load of steel to knock me aside. If anything had happened to you…" He shook his head, then in a low voice, added, "It would have killed me."

"But you would have done the same for me!"

"Yes, but it's my job," he said, then grabbed his sweater and vest and put them back on.

"I won't just stand by and let you get hurt if I can do something to stop it."

There had been no particular emphasis in her voice, and perhaps that was why her simple words cut him to the core. As he gazed into her eyes, he felt something dark stirring inside him. He knew he could take her, right here, right now, but honor demanded more from him.

"I want you. You know that. But we can't keep doing this," Nick said, widening the gap between them.

"Why not? We're both adults," she said, moving toward him.

"Because your real needs go beyond moments, and in the end I'll hurt you. There's a darkness inside me that destroys whatever it touches," he said, moving to the other end of the room, then turning to face her.

"When I look at you, I see the beautiful man you really are, Nick."

"The difference between us is that I've fought too many battles, and I've got too many scars to believe in dreams."

"Do you regret what happened between us?" Drew managed to say, her voice unsteady.

"I wanted you, but I'm not sure you realize the consequences." It was at that very moment that he saw her heart break.

Tears filled her eyes, but, in a heartbeat, anger smothered her pain. "How dare you tell me what I should have done or felt! Do you think I'm incapable of deciding what's right for me just because you were the first man I was with? I made my choice freely. You didn't force me into anything. I'm sorry your ego can't handle the truth."

"I can handle you, and any spin you want to put on what happened between us," Nick said, his voice hard, his eyes boring through her. "I was only trying—"

"To put me on a safe little pedestal, to turn me into someone better loved from afar—mostly because that's what you're comfortable with. That way you can avoid all those complicated emotions that come with caring about someone."

"I care."

As she turned away, he reached out and pulled her back into his arms. His mouth was savage as it took hers, forcing her lips to open and surrender to him. Her tiny whimpers told him that she needed and wanted him, and that knowledge fueled the fires raging inside him.

Dark pleasures began to overwhelm his rational thoughts. Only one thing penetrated that fog—those beeps....

The annoying, insistent sound broke through to him, and he suddenly realized his phone was ringing. Cursing, he moved away from her and answered it. "Yeah," he growled.

"We have no usable prints from the crane, interior or exterior," Travis said. "The real operator was at Petra's, eating lunch, and several people backed up his story. Officers are still canvassing the street, looking for possible witnesses to the incident. I took a dozen or so photos of the construction crew, hoping one of you might recognize a face and give us a lead. I'd send them to you now, but they're really poor quality. I'd like to get to my work station and clean them up a little first, then print them out."

"That makes sense. Where are you?" Nick asked.

"I'm watching the River Walk Campground, but no one's shown up here or at The Painted Dove."

"Can you get someone you trust to cover for you, bro? I'd like those photos ASAP. It would best if we could meet, preferably somewhere away from the station, at a spot where an Anglo would stick out like a sore thumb."

"How about the Harvest Dance at the community center in Rattlesnake," Travis said. "It's tonight."

"Great idea," Nick said. "I'll meet you by Begay's concession stand."

Nick hung up, grabbed his jacket and headed to the door. "Come on. It's time to leave. I'll fill you in on the plan once we get on the road."

"It's really crowded here," Drew said as Nick drove into the graveled parking lot that circled the Rattlesnake community center.

Young people wearing jeans and western-cut shirts, and

older ones wearing the traditional velour shirts and long skirts, were all around them, most heading quickly toward the warmth of the large facility.

"It's a celebration that brings in people from as far away as Gallup and Teec Nos Pos."

Nick led her into the combination basketball gym, auditorium and recreation center—a cinder-block building with a high ceiling. People were laughing, eating and slow-dancing next to the elevated bandstand, where a country and western group was playing.

Nick and Drew stayed close to the wall, easing around the edge of the crowd until they caught up to Travis near a concession stand.

Travis greeted them, and standing below one of the lights, showed his brother the photos.

"None of those fit the guy I saw," Nick said, keeping his arm around Drew's waist, holding her close. Feeling her tense up, he glanced at her. "What's wrong?"

"I'm getting a real bad feeling," she answered, leaning over so he could hear her above the din. "We're being watched. Can't you feel it?"

Nick stopped, and making sure they had their backs to the wall, studied the sea of faces around them.

"What do you want to do now?" Travis asked Nick.

"Look for Anglos." Nick paused for a moment, then smiled slowly. "I've got an idea. My Navajo's a little rusty, but do you remember how to say 'she's dead'?"

Travis smiled. "Excellent plan," he answered, filling in the gaps of Nick's plan. "If I yell that out in Navajo, The People will move back to avoid the *chindi*. The ones left up close will either be Anglo or health workers."

"Exactly," Nick said. "So, can you translate it?"

"There's no direct translation. The closest I can get to it is *bi adin doo holo da*. Basically, that translates to 'she does not exist'," Travis said. "But if there's an Anglo on your tail, he's suddenly going to find himself standing all alone."

"Bro, if she says he's here, you can count on it."

Travis gave Drew a smile. "You may yet get my brother to believe in something he can't see or touch."

"And now back to reality, folks," Nick snapped. "Let's push our way into the middle of the crowd, then do this during the pause between songs."

"Will people hurt themselves trying to get away?" she asked.

"No. It's not like that. They'll head for the exits because they won't want to be around, but it's not a panic type of thing," Travis said.

They worked their way across the room until they were in the thick of the crowd, then, as the final note from the lead guitar ended, Drew clutched her chest and dropped to the floor.

When Travis yelled out the phrase, people quickly stepped back, most turning away, and put distance between themselves and Drew. One solitary Anglo man, wearing a hooded jacket, remained in place, looking confused and trying to figure out what was going on.

"Gotcha," Nick muttered under his breath, closing in on him.

Drew sat up. "I'm okay, everyone. I just slipped!" she told the crowd.

The Anglo man suddenly pulled a knife from his jacket pocket and opened it with a flick of his wrist. The wicked-looking six-inch blade gleamed as he rushed at Drew, but Nick cut him off, barely avoiding a wild swipe of the blade.

The men circled each other, the knife-wielding man slicing the air before him, keeping Nick at a distance. Suddenly, with a cry that made Drew gasp, the man lunged with the knife. Nick grabbed his wrist, twisted, and the knife dropped to the floor. Unarmed, the man spun and tackled Nick to the floor. On his back, Nick twisted side to side, blocking several more punches as they thrashed around, grunting loudly as he moved.

"He needs help!" Drew said, looking at Travis. "His ribs are killing him."

"Naw. He can't shake it off. This is *his* collar. Nick can take him." Glancing back at her, he grinned. "It's a guy thing."

Nick faked a left/right combination, and as the man flinched, Nick slid underneath and swept the man's legs from under him. Pinning him facedown on the floor, Nick quickly cuffed him as Travis picked up the knife.

The crowd drew closer, but their eyes were on Drew, not on Nick and his prisoner.

Travis brought out his badge and held it high as he spoke. "She fainted from hunger. Anyone have a bowl of mutton stew?"

There was some nervous laughter, then the attention shifted to Nick, who turned the handcuffed man over to two tribal police officers.

"I'd like the chance to question the subject," Nick said, as Drew and Travis joined him.

"At the station," one of the officers answered, leading the way outside.

Travis identified himself. "I'd like the chance to ride over with my brother, so we can pool what we've learned about the suspect. It'll help when he's questioned. Could one of your officers bring his Jeep to the station?" Travis held out the keys, pointing out the vehicle at the same time.

"Sure. I'll leave it in a visitor's slot," one of the tribal officers said, taking the keys.

As they walked across the parking lot, Drew thought about Nick. Life had turned him into a warrior who lived only in the moment—a man who was always ready to fight for what he believed in. But his unbreakable bond to the past meant he'd never be free to build a new future for himself.

The knowledge weighed heavily on her. Somewhere along the way, she'd fallen in love with a cop, repeating the mistake her mother and her aunt had made. Loving a man who wore a badge meant dying a little each time he was late, and risking everything that mattered most each and every day. She already knew what it was like to be the one left behind. She wouldn't go through that again. Yet, there was no turning off her heart.

Feeling bewildered at how things had gotten this crazy, she didn't realize Travis was speaking to her.

"You okay?" Travis asked, nudging her slightly as they reached the pickup.

"You should be asking Nick that," she answered, climbing in.

"He's a hundred percent," Travis said, with an easy grin. "A cop that can't take a punch to the jaw needs to find a new job. Right, bro?"

Nick, who'd gone around to the driver's side, guffawed. "I'm fine except for my aching ribs. He never really connected. But that guy had some training at one point or another."

Travis motioned for Drew to slide over to the middle so he could get in as well. "He sure knew how to handle a knife. And he managed to get real close before we spotted him."

"Yeah, and he's good with a pistol, too. I'm ninety percent sure that he's the guy who shot Marc Lassen."

"If he's the one who killed that boy, then he also has at least some of the answers we need," Drew said.

"He probably does, but a professional hit man will know to keep his mouth shut," Nick said. "We'll need to find some leverage."

Nick drove north to the highway, then turned east on the main road, heading toward the police station in Shiprock.

"That man's face was familiar to me, but not from the shooting," Drew said. "I've seen him before. I just can't figure out where."

Both men immediately looked at her. "Is he your stalker?" Nick asked. "From the mall?"

"No. He's too tall. But there's still something about this guy...."

WHEN THEY ARRIVED AT THE Navajo tribal police station, they were waved down the hall to the interview rooms. Leaving Drew by the two-way mirror, Nick and Travis met the Navajo detective who'd just been assigned the case.

After giving Detective Nakai some background on recent incidents, they entered the room. The speaker was on, and Drew could hear them clearly.

"What's your name?" Nick asked, after the prisoner was re-advised of his rights.

"Eric Goodwin," he answered.

"That's what your driver's license says, but Eric Goodwin doesn't exist," Detective Nakai said. "Well, he did once, but he died before his first birthday. Try again."

The suspect sat back and stared at them wordlessly.

"We'll have the answers soon enough," Detective Nakai said. "You've tried to burn off your fingerprints, but we'll be running you through a facial-recognition program. I'm guessing we'll be getting a hit before too long."

"Knock yourself out," the man replied, with a smile.

"How long have you been tailing me?" Nick asked.

"Why? You want to believe you're not as big a screwup as you really are?"

Nick reached across the table for him, but Travis pulled his brother back.

"Tsk, tsk. Such manners," the man said. "And you call yourself a Marine? Show a little dignity."

Nick stepped away from Travis, his focus on the suspect again. "You know who I am?"

"Oh yeah. You're the hero Marine. Tell me how many real Americans got blown away so you could wear some ribbons on your chest? Sounds to me like all you did was set them up to die."

Nick's expression didn't change. "What about you—any medals, or just a police record?"

"Hey, I figured you, of all people, would know a lot more about me."

"Do we have a personal beef I don't know about?"

"None of my work is personal. I was hired to follow you and that's what I've been doing for the past few days."

"Hired by whom?" Nakai pressed.

"Don't know, don't care. Money's money."

"How did you get paid?" Travis pushed.

"Cash? Offshore bank account? You'll never know."

"What exactly *were* you paid to do—besides kill Marc Lassen?" Nick demanded. The prisoner never even blinked.

"Who?" he answered, at long last.

Nick slammed his fist down so hard on the table it actually shook, despite being bolted down. He wasn't angry, he'd wanted to rattle the suspect. Instead, all the man did was roll his eyes.

"You know who I'm talking about," Nick yelled.

"No. Actually, I don't. But I think it's time for me to stop cooperating. An attorney's on his way here. You can direct your questions at him."

"We're done. Might as well process him," Nick told Nakai. "The county D.A. will have a stack of charges by morning."

As Detective Nakai escorted the prisoner past her, Drew studied his face closely.

"Have you figured out where you've seen him before?" Nick asked.

She shook her head. "He's nobody I see routinely, but I *have* seen him, and not too long ago. I'm sure of it."

Before they could reach the exit, Detective Nakai called out, then jogged down the hall to join them.

"His fingers are so clean, it's got to be the work of acid.

But we found one distinguishing mark. It's an almost imperceptible scar on his left index finger," Nakai said.

"It runs diagonally?" Nick asked, instantly.

The officer nodded. "Yeah. How did you know?"

"I didn't, but before I got put on this case, I was working to ID an arms dealer who operates in this area—calls himself Coyote. The one dependable lead I got was that the dealer's cleanup boy was a guy without prints. My informant said that he did whatever his boss wanted done—wet work, black bag jobs, explosives, the whole nine yards."

"Every law enforcement agency in the state is looking for Coyote. The guy we've got in custody works for him?"

"Yeah. I'll have to call this in to my own people. It's clear now that there's a connection between my original investigation and what's been happening to Drew. She's in the middle of this somehow. But they went after her before she and I ever met."

"There must be another connection between you two, then. You've got to figure out what that is," Travis said.

Seeing Nick looking to her, she shook her head and shrugged. As far as she was concerned, the most important connection between them was one of the heart.

"You're missing something, and eventually, that's going to get you both killed, unless you can find answers," Travis said.

"Our first priority is staying alive. Everything else comes in second," Nick said, heading to the door.

Chapter Twenty

As Drew settled into the passenger seat of the pickup, she gasped. "My laptop's gone."

"This can't have happened here at the station. And for the suspect to have taken it from the truck means he followed us to Rattlesnake. But I watched for a tail, and there was no one back there. I'd stake my life on it."

"You have," Travis said, softly, from where he stood beside the driver's door.

"Bro, there's only one road leading to Rattlesnake from the east, and you *know* I would've spotted a tail. I'm not one to lower my guard, on- or off-duty."

Nick glanced at an indeterminate point ahead, lost in thought. "This may have been the work of another thief altogether—somebody working the Rattlesnake parking lot tonight."

"One who left no trace of the theft?" Travis shook his head. "I think the suspect planned all along to take the laptop first, then neutralize both of you later at the dance, making it look like a random attack. I'd bet he was hoping that no one would ever notice the laptop was missing. It sure sounds like the work of the suspect we've got in custody—Coyote's man."

Drew suppressed a shudder. "Neutralizing" sounded better than "murdering," but the fact was that they both came down to the same thing—death. "So, if you're right, my laptop's in his car, wherever it is."

"Tribal officers are searching for his vehicle, but until the dance is over and the cars and trucks clear out, they may not make any serious progress," Travis said.

"But, guys, here's the real question. Why would anyone want my computer? There's nothing on it that would be of any interest to anyone."

"Since the crime points back to the guy without fingerprints, what have you added recently that might be important to a criminal like Coyote?" Nick asked her.

"Nothing. I added a few new titles to my list of good reads, but there's nothing threatening about a librarian recommending books."

After Travis left for the Jeep, Nick pulled out of the tribal police parking lot. "There's a link between you and me, Drew. All the evidence points to it. But I'm out of ideas," he admitted.

She started to answer, when Nick's phone rang.

Nick put it on speaker and they both heard Detective Nakai's voice at the other end. "We found the suspect's car," he said. "It was parked in a private driveway about a quarter mile from the community center. One of the families walking home from the dance noticed a strange car in their neighbor's driveway and heard the TV going. The elderly woman who lived there usually went to bed early, so they took a closer look and found the front door open and the resident dead on the living room floor. The crime scene unit was dispatched, and when they checked out the car, they found the laptop with Ms. Simmons's name. A program erasing all the files was still running, apparently. An officer turned it off."

"I'm heading back right now," Nick said, checking the rearview mirror, then pulling over to the side of the road.

"I'm en route to that location myself," Nakai said, giving them directions to the crime scene.

Nick turned the pickup around and headed back west.

ON THE DRIVE WEST TO Rattlesnake, they compared the details of their day-to-day routines. After a while, it was clear that, except for the facts that she'd been training for a job at the police station, and he was a detective there, they had nothing else in common. Nick slammed his hand on the wheel. "It's *got* to have something to do with the department. That's our only connection."

Ten minutes later, they drove past the deserted-looking community center, now illuminated by a single light over the main entrance. Ahead lay a residential area. The flashing red-and-blue lights from the police vehicles led them to the scene. As they parked, they saw a nondescript gold sedan in a driveway, caught between two arrays of floodlights.

Detective Nakai came over to greet them. "I'd like both of you to take a look at the vic before they take the body away. I need to know if either of you have met her before."

As Drew followed the detective up the drive, she noted that the closest neighbors were on their front steps, watching from at least a hundred yards away.

Almost as if he'd read her mind, Nick said, "The house will be boarded up, and no one will live here again. It'll probably be torn down by an Anglo wrecking company. Even our modernists won't tempt the *chindi*."

"But if they're modernists, why would they care?"

"Think of it this way. Most Anglos don't believe that walking under a ladder is bad luck, but given a choice, they'll still walk around it."

As they approached the front door, they met two men wheeling a body encased in a plastic bag down the sidewalk on a gurney. The men stopped as Detective Nakai signaled them.

Every muscle in Drew's body tensed as one of the men opened the zipper several inches so that the floodlights captured the woman's face.

Drew studied the face of the elderly Navajo woman. "I don't know her," she managed to say, in a strangled voice.

"I've never seen her before either," Nick said.

"From the angle of the head at the scene, and the relative absence of bruises, I'd guess that her neck was broken," Nakai said. "It was a quick death. She probably never knew what hit her."

"But she didn't deserve this," Drew whispered.

"No, she did not. But I'm betting that we already have her killer behind bars, and that's where he's going to stay," Nakai said. "The booking officer has given him a nickname based on the fact that he has no fingerprints. Until we get a real ID, we're calling him Slick."

Nick nodded. "Fits."

As the body was taken away, Nakai led them up the drive. "When we opened the trunk of the sedan we found some firearms, including an M-16 assault rifle. We're hoping to match bullets from that weapon to the ones used to kill the Las Cruces police officer. There were burglary tools in there, too, including a set of special keys and a small rubber mallet, the kind burglars use for bumping locks."

"He's probably the same guy who broke into Ms. Simmons's apartment and a Three Rivers bakery the other night," Nick said. "Did you find anything else?"

"As a matter of fact, yes. There's a GPS locator attached to the console," he said, taking them over to the sedan. "You mentioned something about suspecting a tail?" Nick nodded. "We can switch it on and see if anything on you is giving away your position."

"That's a real good idea, detective."

As the locator switch came on, their current address

popped up on the screen. "Move around. Let's eliminate your clothing," Nakai suggested.

Nick and Drew walked away from each other, but nothing changed on the locator's screen.

"It can't be our wheels," Nick said. "That's my brother's pickup. The sender has to be keying on something else."

"It can't be my laptop either. He had it with him," Drew said.

"If it isn't the truck, maybe it's something inside it, something you've been carrying around. A jacket, maybe? Or a purse?" Nakai suggested.

It took about ten minutes, but by a meticulous process of elimination, they were finally able to narrow the signal emitter down to one object.

Drew shook her head. "That can't be right. That's a reference manual from the police department's library. The information is primarily for the clerical staff."

Nick took the cloth-bound book from her and studied it. There didn't seem to be anything particularly noteworthy about it, and the pages appeared to be intact.

"There aren't any bumps on the front and back covers," Nakai said, also studying it, "and you flipped through the pages. Nobody cut a hole in there for a transmitter."

"That leaves the spine," Drew said.

Nick twisted the front and back of the book and tore the pages away from the spine. A slender green-and-silver circuit board suddenly fell out, but Drew caught it before it hit the ground.

Drew stared at the device resting in the palm of her hand, then Detective Nakai picked it up with glove-encased fingers and dropped it into an evidence bag.

"This doesn't make any sense," Drew said, watching as Nakai wrote the required information on the bag's label.

"Who gave you this particular book?" Nick asked.

"Beth Michaels. It was the same one she used when she was learning the new database system."

"Did Beth need anyone's permission to take the book?" Nick asked.

"I have no idea. And I don't know where it was kept before that. She loaned it to me, and I accepted it gratefully. It's what I've been using to practice."

"Hold that thought." Nick turned to Nakai. "Were there any serial numbers on the weapons you found?"

"They'd been filed down, but our tech said he'll probably be able to restore them. We have a new process that works really well."

"All right. You have my cell number. Give me a call if you get a hit on any of the numbers, or if you get an ID on Slick."

"No problem," Nakai said.

"Do you have any idea when I'll be able to get my computer back?" Drew asked Nakai.

"It may be a while. Our computer tech is in Window Rock for the next few days, and we need him to try to restore your hard drive. If nothing's been overwritten, most of the files can be restored. Maybe then we can find out why Slick erased everything you had."

"If I can get the proper software, I can restore those files a lot sooner than that. Detective Blacksheep would be right there with me, too, so if he saw something he thought you'd find useful, he'd be able to transmit the information to you right away."

Nakai looked at Blacksheep. "I'll have to get permission, and you'd have to sign for it."

"Do it," Nick said.

LESS THAN FIVE MINUTES LATER, they were on their way, Nick at the wheel.

The laptop sat on the floorboards, between Drew's feet.

"You and I have to talk with Beth," Nick said.

"At this hour?" She glanced at her watch. "It's two in the morning."

"We'll catch her at breakfast before she goes into work."

"Beth's a fine, honest woman, Nick. There's no way I'm going to believe that she's involved in anything illegal."

"Medical bills can leave you in the hole, even with the city's health insurance plan. That could make her more susceptible to corruption."

"If you think she took a bribe and sold us out, you're nuts. Beth and Slick working for the same person? No way, not now, not ever."

Nick called the Three River's station next, making sure that the information they had on crimes that may have involved Slick was sent to Detective Nakai's office.

"What bothers me most are the little things I can't make sense of, like why my Web page was hacked and deleted," Drew said. "Hacked…well, that's something that happens to a lot of people, and it's usually used to embarrass a person or take it over for something illegal or disgusting. But to delete it entirely, what's the point?"

"Have you been able to recall precisely what you had on it? Anything that may have slandered or embarrassed anyone, for instance?"

"There was nothing like that on it," she said, firmly. "I have a few hours of computer work ahead of me, trying to restore my hard drive, and while I'm doing that, I'll also try to remember some of the missing details that were part of my original web page. Once I've got everything back up and running, you can take a look and judge for yourself."

Chapter Twenty-One

Drew sat alone in Nick's living room, working on her laptop. Obviously, something about her Web page had threatened whoever was after her, but she had no idea why. Her blog had held her dreams and plans for the future, as well as insights into her current life juggling two jobs. It was the kind of thing that might interest friends, but certainly not anything that would create a controversy of any kind.

Nick walked in moments later. "I just got off the phone with Nakai. The tribal police managed to recover two sets of serial numbers. They match weapons that were confiscated by our department and logged into evidence months ago."

Drew stared at him in shock. "But those stay behind lock and key in the station's evidence room. How did they find their way back out into the street? Aren't weapons that can't be traced back to legitimate owners, or are no longer part of an investigation, eventually destroyed?"

"Yes, especially automatic assault rifles like the M-16. Every two years, the chief takes the weapons to Albuquerque and the county bomb squad blows them to pieces. But obviously, that's not what happened with these guns. Somehow, they leaked out of the system and into the hands of dirt bags like Slick. My guess is that Coyote's behind this operation."

"So someone's been smuggling arms out of the evidence room, filing down their serial numbers, then reselling them to the bad guys," she said. "That same person—Coyote, or his department-connected thief—could have been the one responsible for putting the transmitter in my reference book. But here's something I don't get. Shouldn't the evidence room clerk have noticed that guns were missing?"

"Anyone with access to the evidence is suspect, but once the tribal police's report is out, whoever stole those weapons is going to scramble to cover things up and remove any damning evidence."

"Is there any way to slow down the release of that report and buy some time?"

He nodded. "I'm already on that. My brother has a high-placed friend in the tribal PD, and he's agreed to hold off filing the report for another twenty-four hours. But that's all the time we've got."

"I wonder if that's the reason I became a target—they assumed, or maybe were told, that I'd eventually be overseeing the evidence room records."

Nick shook his head. "To go after you solely on the assumption that you might figure things out someday doesn't add up. These people are too good at covering their tracks," he said. "Our best shot at catching them is to set a trap. Once we have a suspect in custody, we'll get our answers."

"Like how I fit into this," Drew said, with a nod. "So what now?"

"We need to put the kind of weapon in the evidence room that's bound to be high on Coyote's shopping list." Nick sat back and rubbed his chin. "I have just the thing, too. A deployed buddy of mine somehow managed to ship home a disassembled AK-47 he 'liberated'. It's illegal, fully automatic, and virtually untraceable. After he got married, his wife refused to have the weapon in the house, so he brought it to me and asked me to destroy it."

"He knew it was illegal, so he took it to a cop?" she asked, surprised.

"It was during one of those amnesty periods. And remember, he brought it to me, not to the station."

"But you kept it?" she asked, still trying to understand.

"It hasn't been that long."

"Okay, so we use that as bait. But how do we get it into the evidence room?"

"I'll need to fill out some paperwork, but that's easy enough. Then I'll have Koval take it in."

"Do you think he'll do things your way?"

"In most cases, he'd rather set himself on fire," Nick joked, "but when there's evidence that a cop's gone bad, everyone's perspective changes. We all want to nail him—or her."

TIRED, BUT EXCITED BY the prospect of finally being able to identify her tormentor, Drew only managed a few hours sleep on Nick's couch. Hearing a clinking sound, she stirred awake and sat up. Nick was seated on the floor across the room, assembling the Russian-designed assault rifle.

"Get some rest?" he asked.

"Some. What time is it?"

"Time to get going. We'll grab breakfast, make one quick stop, and be in town by seven. That's assuming I get the right response from Koval," Nick said, standing. He'd been wearing evidence gloves while working, careful not to leave a fingerprint of his own.

"I'm going to call Koval now," he said, reaching for his cell phone. "Get ready to leave while I talk to him."

Less than ten minutes later, they were on the road. The AK-47, one of the most effective military firearms on the planet, was wrapped in a bath towel, behind the seat of the truck.

"How are we going to know when someone takes the bait and tries to remove this gun from evidence?"

"I've got that covered. I made a call before you woke up, and arranged to meet with someone who can provide me with a tracking device that's not department issue. The guy is a private detective who runs his own business."

A short time later, they arrived at an upscale home on the mesa, just outside Three Rivers.

"Hey, buddy." The tall Anglo man greeted them at the door, then immediately glanced at Drew, giving her a quick once-over.

Nick introduced them. "Drew Simmons, this is Dennis Fields."

Dennis shook hands with her, but obviously aware of Navajo customs, didn't offer to shake Nick's. "I've been keeping up on events. Somebody's really testing you this time, Nick," he said, taking them into the den. The room held three large, overstuffed leather couches and several matching chairs.

Nick didn't comment. He had no idea how much Dennis really knew. One established technique for eliciting information was pretending to know far more than you did. People assumed you were already familiar with the facts and spoke much more freely than they normally would.

"Relax, buddy," Dennis said, reading Nick's expression. "I have a secure contact on the tribal PD who exchanges information with me from time to time. That's how I got the latest about Coyote and those weapons."

Nick expelled his breath in a hiss. "That information shouldn't have gotten out, even to you."

"My buddy and I served overseas in the same national guard unit. We're like brothers. He knew that I work with the Three Rivers PD on occasion, and wanted me to know something was off there, so I'd watch my back."

"Yeah, I hear you." Bonds formed during wartime often stayed with a person for life.

Dennis offered them a seat on one of the sofas before settling into an easy chair. "So what kind of tracking device are you looking for?"

"I want something that's state of the art, and its signal

emitter has got to be as small as possible," Nick said. "I plan on hiding it inside a metal device—nonelectronic, that is."

"Not a problem," Dennis answered. "I've got just the thing. It's not only powerful, it's also reliable. How long will you need it?"

"I'm not sure. It's for a case I'm working on for the PD, but I can't give you any more details than that."

Dennis went into the next room and returned holding a button-size transmitter and a tracking device the size of a deck of cards. "Here you go. This thing won't let you down. The batteries are good for three months, more if kept under room-temperature conditions."

"Thanks," Nick said, standing up.

"Find the piece of crap who's selling out the Three Rivers PD before the bad smell gets on everyone."

Nick nodded. "That's the plan."

THEY PULLED OFF THE ROAD AT A rest stop on the outskirts of town. Wearing latex gloves to avoid leaving fingerprints, Nick hollowed out a small recess for the tracking device in the stock of the AK-47.

"The only way anyone will see the emitter is if they dismantle the weapon, and that isn't necessary to verify it's in working condition," Nick said. He wrapped the rifle in the towel once again and placed it behind the seat.

"Now we find Koval?" she asked.

"Yes, and when we get there, stay in the car. I'll talk to him. I don't want you involved. If we have a dirty cop, our own brotherhood will find him."

She nodded, understanding, and remembering her father's and uncle's pride in the department. No one would rest until honor was restored.

Thirty minutes passed before they met with Koval in front of an empty house with a for-sale sign on the dried-out lawn. Koval looked around to make sure they weren't being watched, an unlikely possibility considering the neighbor-hood was part of an abandoned development. "This better work."

"It will." Nick handed Koval the wrapped AK-47 along with the paperwork and the GPS receiver.

As they walked to Koval's sedan, Drew was no longer able to hear their conversation. Although she knew officers closed ranks when something like this happened, she found herself wishing Nick would share more of his world with her. But this was a side of his life she knew he'd always keep locked away. And maybe that was a good thing. They'd grown too close, and heartbreak was sure to follow when it all finally came to an end.

When Nick climbed back behind the wheel, he glanced over at her. "We're done here. Koval will monitor the bug."

She stared out the window. "I'm still trying to figure out where I fit into all this. I don't have a vested interest in what the department does or doesn't do. Yet, here I am."

Nick nodded. "You're connected in some way. The deleted Web page...do you think you can reconstruct it completely now?"

"I'm almost there. Let's go back to your place and I'll try to finish it up."

Matters seemed to be coming together in a rush. That knowledge bit into her hard. Though she'd never regret the time they'd spent together, intuition assured her that a piece of her heart would remain behind when it came time for her to move on and say goodbye. But as she'd known all along, some things were never meant to be.

ONCE AT NICK'S HOME, she sat at the table with her laptop and tried to recall every detail of her Web page. As she worked, she could hear Nick and Travis in the gym, arguing. Although she tried to block their words out and concentrate on what she was doing, it was difficult not to listen in.

"There's a *hataalii* I know who can do an Enemy Way for you, bro. You haven't had a full night's sleep since our unit returned stateside, and you're exhausted. You have a future in the making now, but if you don't settle the past—"

"I can't think about this right now. I've got a case," Nick roared.

"You *always* have a case," Travis snapped. "Look at yourself. You don't even heal as fast as you should because of the added weight you carry—all from a false sense of responsibility."

One of them closed the door, and their voices faded. She sighed, curious about what they were saying, but knowing she had other responsibilities now.

Drew stared at the screen and focused on her restoration project. Searching through her image files, she remembered that sometime back she'd made an album to share her special family photos with friends.

She tried to duplicate it now, going through the various archived images. She smiled as her gaze fell on the old, slightly faded wedding photos of her mom and dad. Her mother's expression, as she looked at her new husband, spoke softly to Drew, telling her something she'd never realized before. Her mother hadn't married a cop—she'd followed her heart and married a man she couldn't live without.

Drew looked at the next photo. That one had been taken a few months prior to her father's death. In it, her mother was leaning back against her husband's chest, gazing up at him. His arms were wrapped around her, and the look in her mother's eyes spoke of an enduring love, one strong enough to withstand life's many trials.

Despite all their troubles, her mother had loved the man she'd chosen, faults and all, to the very end. There were no regrets on her face, just the contentment of a woman who'd known both the cost and the wonder of love.

Drew wiped the tears that ran down her face, but not before Nick walked into the room.

Crouching by her side, he took her hand gently. "What's wrong?"

"I always thought my father had made my mother's life a hell on earth," she whispered. "I saw Dad as a man who was married to his work—and Mom took the leftovers. But I was wrong about them. The truth is right there in those old photos. There's a lot more to my mom and dad's story than I ever realized."

"Law enforcement *can* get under a man's skin. But that doesn't mean that there's nothing left at the end of the day. Love is sometimes the only thing that keeps a man from losing himself," Nick said.

As she saw herself reflected in the warmth of his eyes, the pull between them overwhelmed all caution. She touched the side of his face in a gentle caress and decided to tell him what was in her heart. Just then, Travis came into the room.

Looking at both of them, he grinned. "Should I have knocked?"

Nick glared at his brother.

Embarrassed, Drew focused back on the computer. "I've done all I can to reconstruct my page. It's still not exact, but the bulk of it is there."

"What's missing?" Nick asked, pressing her.

"A few photos I'd downloaded straight from my cell phone, but there's nothing remarkable about any of those. They were mostly quick shots of me shopping and showing off things I bought, like a scarf and some shoes I thought were cute."

"Put those up on the screen," Nick said.

She did as he asked. "See? Nothing spectacular, just stuff I was sharing with my friends."

"Make that image larger," Nick said, his eyes riveted on one of the photos. "Now clear up the background and add flash, so we can get a good look at those people in the background."

She did as he asked, then gasped. Standing by the specialty coffee kiosk was Chief Franklin having coffee with two men. One of them was Slick. She didn't recognize the third man.

"That's the same guy in the photo my contact gave me. That's Coyote," Nick said.

"Now it makes sense," Drew said. "Once I started working at the station, the men figured it would only be a matter of time before I saw Coyote's photo. They couldn't take a chance that I'd put things together. I held the key linking Coyote to Chief Franklin."

Nick nodded. "Yeah, it makes sense. But we still need proof. All we really have here is a photo of the chief drinking coffee with some guys. He could claim that they shared a table and a brief conversation."

"So what do we do now?" she asked.

"We talk to Beth Michaels. Let's see if she can tell us how that tracking device got into your manual."

After learning that Beth had taken the morning off, Nick and Drew left for her house.

"You and Travis have made a wonderful home for yourselves," she said on the way to town. "It's got everything two guys could ever want."

"It lacks...pink," he answered, with a grin.

"No it doesn't," she said, laughing. "It's the perfect place for the two of you."

"True, it fits us," he conceded. "We made it that way, just as you did with your apartment. That's *your* perfect fit."

She shook her head. "My apartment was never a real home. It was more of a...transition place."

"How do you define home?"

"A few weeks ago I would have said that home was a place of security and safety, the center of life well lived."

"And now?"

"Home shouldn't be static. It should be an ever evolving place, tailored to fit changing needs. The heart of it should remain the same—a place of sanctuary that's far more than wood and stucco. But home could be a tent, or even on wheels. What makes it home is that sense of place and feeling of peace the people inside give to it."

He said nothing for several long moments. "Peace and security weren't things I ever had, so I never missed them. I went after the opposite. I wanted the adrenaline rush that comes from facing uncertainty and danger. That's why I became a Marine, and later a cop."

"There's room for both in someone's life, isn't there?"

"For some men, yes, but I'd never trust the things you spoke about. It's when you're comfortable and sure of your future that life comes in and blindsides you. I care about making the most of today. Tomorrow can't be predicted."

His answer saddened her because she knew they'd never share a common dream. A part of Nick's heart would continue to be weighed down by his past. Trying to silence the ache inside her, she looked out the window at the passing cars.

They arrived at Beth's twenty minutes later. "You should take the lead here, Drew. You know her as a friend, which means you're more likely to get straight answers."

"Let me see what I can do," she said.

The house smelled of disinfectant and medications, something they detected the moment Beth answered the door. Drew suppressed a shudder.

Beth waved Nick and Drew to chairs around the kitchen table. "I'm surprised to see you guys here. What's up?"

"Beth, we have reason to believe that someone in the department set me up from the very beginning," Drew said, telling her of the homing device in the manual. "What made you choose that particular book?"

Beth gave her a hard look. "And unless I come up with an answer that satisfies you, you'll think I'm responsible and working with whoever set you up?" Beth shook her head. "None of what has happened to you is my doing."

"I know that because I know you, Beth. But I believe someone used you. Think back. What made you choose that particular manual?"

Beth sat back and stared at something indeterminate across the room. "I went into the library section of records one afternoon and saw Chief Franklin and Captain Wright. I mentioned that I was trying to find a good reference book that would help with our software and Captain Wright asked me what *I'd* used. That's when I remembered the green book. That's what we called it. I couldn't find a copy there, but Chief Franklin mentioned that he had one in his bookcase, and he brought it to me later that afternoon."

"Did you ever tell him who it was for?" Nick asked.

"I'm not sure." Beth met Nick's gaze. "I know you think that medical bills make me vulnerable to corruption. I'll admit, even my part of the copay is steep. But my financial troubles are temporary. My husband's life insurance policy will ultimately take care of all that, and provide well for me for the rest of my days. So where's my motive, Detective Blacksheep?"

Nick looked at her. "We already have a good idea who's behind this—a dirty cop."

"So how can I help you?" she asked, without hesitation.

"Can you get us the security video feed from the evidence room?"

"I can access anything in records, including the images, but I can't do it from home. Anything *that* sensitive has to originate from a work station inside our departmental network, one that's physically connected to the system. It's set up with its own firewall, unlike the case files that officers can access from their vehicles with their MDTs or personal laptops, using the proper passwords."

"Would you be willing to call it a training session and take us over there right now?" Drew asked.

"If I do that during the day, it'll be too easy for us to get caught, even in my private office. And I can't leave Charlie at night. There's no one else here to take care of him."

Drew nodded. "I have an idea. We could get into those records from any station terminal using your password. Is that right?"

"But doing something like that could also land you in jail."

"I know. It's a risk."

"And not just for you," Beth said. "If you access those records using my password, you'll be leaving my calling card."

"We don't have another choice," Nick said. "We have a bad cop, and we need to bring him out into the open."

"All right. I'm the wife of a thirty-year cop, and the department still means a lot to him, and to me. Keeping it clean is worth the risk."

Beth took a steadying breath and looked at both of them. "I won't tell you my password, but no one can blame me if you end up guessing it." Looking at Drew, she added, "It's time for me to check on Charlie. He's always been the center of my life. We're the same age, both of us born in 1945, and I think that's why we've always had so much in common."

Drew nodded to Beth. "Thanks for everything." Looking at Nick, she stood and gestured to the door. "Let's go. We have all we need."

Moments later, as they set out, Nick kept a close eye on the rearview mirror. "There won't be any turning back once we start this operation, Drew. You'll be in too deep. You're risking everything, and not just your job. Are you sure you're ready?"

She nodded. "Someone else started this, but this librarian's going to finish it."

Chapter Twenty-Two

The evening shift was on duty by the time they entered the station. At night, the department had an edgier feel to it. A different type of criminal came through the doors then, and the entire place resonated with the dangers that thrived in darkness.

Beth's private office was away from the records room and down a hall that wasn't fully covered by surveillance cameras. Leading the way inside and leaving the light off, Drew took Beth's chair, and turned on her work station and monitor.

"Close the door," she whispered to Nick. "We don't want to attract any extra attention."

Drew kept her fingers on the keyboard and entered "1945" then the word "Charlie." The onscreen message read, "incorrect password."

"Try Charlie, then 1945," he suggested.

She did, but got the same results.

"Do you think she gave us the wrong password? Maybe we've been set up," Nick said.

Drew leaned back and stared at the screen, lost in thought. "She said that Charlie was the center of her life. I thought she was just telling me how she felt, but I think it was more than that." Drew typed "19," then Charlie, and finally "45." "Bingo. We're in."

Using the mouse, she accessed the icon for the security

cameras, then clicked on the evidence-room images, which were automatically recorded onto a hard drive.

"These cameras store years of data. They're on every minute of every day, and it's all carefully archived. This could take hours, days," she said, as Nick came to look over her shoulder. "We need to narrow the time frame."

"So how do we speed it up?"

"Give me the serial number of one of the weapons we know were snatched from the evidence room. I can open a window and do a records search. That'll list when the weapon was logged into the system."

Once she had a start date to begin the visual search, Drew scrolled through the video that recorded the hours following the placement of the M-16 assault rifle into storage.

Seeing a flicker in the feed, Drew suddenly stopped it, then ran it back, frame by frame. "Five minutes are missing," she said. "There's a gap in the time stamp. Someone either turned off the cameras, or all four of them stopped working at once."

"Not likely. All the electronics in this station have battery backups, too," Nick said. "Run it back again."

Drew did as he asked, then pointed to the monitor. "Did you see that?" she asked, freezing the image.

"What?" Nick asked.

"I was watching the weapons rack, the one with the long-barreled guns. Watch the guns on the right as I take the feed from the moment right before the gap to the time immediately afterwards."

Drew played through the sequence again, flipping back and forth. Some of the weapons jumped slightly from left or right, and two of them changed lengths in the before and after images.

"That M-16 rifle was replaced by another similar weapon while the cameras were shut off," Nick said. "The barrel's longer now. Someone switched the guns."

But there were more glitches in the recoding system. In every instance, the evidence-room clerk on duty had been on break, or out to lunch. During that time, someone replaced the guns there with lookalikes that could pass the scrutiny of a casual observer.

"At least we know who isn't guilty. The evidence-room clerk has no direct access to those security cameras," Nick said. "There are only two people who have access to both the room and the cameras, so that narrows it down. The way I see it, this had to have been done by either Captain Wright or Chief Franklin...or maybe both."

"Progress. Now all we have to do is get out of the station without attracting attention."

They were halfway down the hall when they heard Chief Franklin reaming out an officer for screwing up a report.

Nick pulled her back quickly into the darkened hall. "We can't leave the station right now. If Franklin sees us walking past the bullpen, we won't have a leg to stand on."

Just then, around the corner of the hall, she heard the desk sergeant greet Travis.

Nick whistled a few notes.

"What are you doing? You're going to give us away!"

"Whistling in a place filled with good ol' boys won't even raise an eyebrow," he said, then heard the answering strains. "Good. He's coming."

"Was that some special kind of signal between you two?"

"It goes all the way back to when we were kids. If one of us got in trouble, the other would be there to help. We had our own signals and codes...." His voice trailed off as he heard footsteps.

Travis came around the corner and grinned at his brother. "It's a good thing that you and I joined the same PD, bro. You'd have been lost without me."

"Dream on. You still owe me for saving your butt a few

times at the police academy. Now I'm collecting. I need a way out, one that doesn't take me right past the chief. If he sees me here, it's going to hit the fan, and I can't exactly explain what we've been up to."

"The weight room is usually empty this time of night," Travis started, then shook his head. "No, wait. There's that civilian self-defense class going on right now. However, you could pass through without raising an eyebrow, and a little later, if Drew walks in, the instructor will assume she signed up. She could stay for the class, then exit with the others when it's over, out the back."

"No way. We can't afford to waste that much time. And what if Franklin decides to look in on the session, like he does sometimes, and spots Drew—without me?"

Hearing a commotion down the hall, Drew peered around the corner and saw three ladies of the evening being booked. Some of the male suspects that had been brought in on other charges were whistling and making off-color suggestions.

"I have an idea," Drew said quickly. "You can go through the weight room like your brother suggested. Then you," she said, looking at Travis, "can pretend to have arrested me, then offered me a deal, providing I identify my pimp. With a cover story like that, we'll be able to go right past the other women out front, and step out the door."

"You're not dressed the part," Travis said, shaking his head. "You'll stand out."

"We can make it work. I just have to make sure no one looks at my face," she said, then glanced inside one of the open offices. "I'll need a pair of scissors...and your pullover," she added, looking at Nick.

He protested, but she insisted, pointing out that they were out of options.

Nick stripped off his pullover, then handed it to her. "Now what?" he asked, putting his leather jacket back on and zipping it up.

"Give me a few minutes," she said, ducking into an open office and closing the door behind her.

THREE MINUTES LATER, after doing some extensive scissoring work on her wardrobe, she emerged and tossed Nick her ballistic vest. Instead of jeans, she was now wearing supershort shorts, with a dropped waistline that exposed her belly button. She'd also recut what had been Nick's pullover, so that it sported a low neckline and tied directly below her breasts. Her lipstick was on extra thick as well.

Travis stared at her for a moment, his gaze taking her in from top to bottom. "I've decided to give you a run for your money, bro."

"Don't go there," Nick growled, then glared at Drew. "What do you think you're doing?"

"No one's going to be looking at my face while I'm wearing this cheesy outfit. Your brother will be able to escort me out the door easily."

"She's got a point," Travis said. "But I'll have to handcuff you."

Nick pushed him aside. "I'll do it. Give me the cuffs."

Nick placed them around her wrists and adjusted them so they weren't too tight. "All right. You're all set."

Drew turned around, just a foot away now, and had to bite back a smile. Nick's expression, a mixture of possessiveness and desire, spoke louder than words ever could have. He wanted her, and that knowledge made her feel powerfully feminine. More important, it also gave her the confidence she needed to complete what she started.

As Nick turned and walked down the hall, Travis grasped her arm, then urged her to the exit. "Keep looking down, and I'll lead you past the bullpen as fast as I can."

Taking advantage of the confusion still surrounding the booking desk, Travis slipped through the noisy group. Although she got some wolf whistles, no one, including Chief Franklin, glanced at her face.

Less than a minute later, Nick met them outside. "Here you go, bro, safe and sound," Travis said, unfastening her cuffs.

"You okay, Drew?" Nick asked, taking off his leather jacket and placing it over her shoulders.

She slipped her arms into the jacket, feeling his warmth and enjoying his scent. As she glanced up to thank him, the look on Nick's face made her breath catch in her throat. No one had ever looked at her like that. Heat spiraled inside her, making her ache for him. Although Nick had taken all her ideas of what she'd wanted her future to be like and flipped them upside down, the pull to follow her heart was stronger than ever.

"Time to get out of here," Nick said.

As the truck roared to life, she thought about Travis and his passion for these kinds of toys. He would be a handful for some woman someday. The Blacksheep brothers... They were a family like no other she'd ever known.

They'd driven about a mile when Nick's cell phone rang.

"I've been monitoring the tracking device and the AK's on the move," Koval said. "It's in Chief Franklin's car, but I can't absolutely confirm that Chief Franklin's driving."

"What's your heading?"

"North on Pine Street."

"Stay on him," Nick said, then punching another number, called Travis. "Has Chief Franklin left the station?"

"Yeah. He stormed out of here less than five minutes ago."

"Did you see him leave?"

"No. I just heard some of the officers grousing after he left. Apparently the chief's decided to retire. Word has it that he got another job offer."

"Interesting timing," Nick said. "How about backing us up on the takedown? I'll fill you in when you get here."

"So it's the chief?" Travis asked.

"Sure looks like it," Nick replied, and gave Travis their location.

No sooner than he'd hung up, Koval called back.

"Chief Franklin's car is now parked on Bosque Road, but I'm too far back to get a good look."

"We're en route to back you up," he said.

Nick updated his brother and then filled Drew in. "I want to catch Chief Franklin with the goods, but in situations like these things can go wrong fast. You'll need to do as I say—no arguments. Our lives may depend on it."

"All right—with one exception." She saw him clench his jaw. "Don't expect me to run off and leave you if you need help."

"Don't you *ever* do what you're told?"

"No."

He expelled his breath in a hiss. There were millions of available women out in the world. Why had he fallen in love with Drew? The woman was impossible. She insisted on questioning even the most simple of requests. Ever since she'd come into his life, nothing had gone according to his plan.

As he glanced over at her, she gave him a gentle smile and the gesture blasted through his defenses.

Exasperated, he clenched his hands around the steering wheel, unclenched them, then tightened his grip again. She was impossible to deal with, but he knew one thing: his life would never be complete without her.

"Are you okay?" she asked, eyeing him closely.

"I'm fine," he growled. Along with his heart, he'd obviously lost what was left of his mind.

Chapter Twenty-Three

As they drove down Bosque Road, Nick could see Koval's car, parked by the side of the road. "Call Koval and tell him we're here."

Drew took the phone and did as he asked. "All I'm getting is voicemail."

"Something's wrong. Let's see what we're up against, then we'll call Travis and give him our new location."

Nick drove by Koval's unmarked car at the posted speed. No one was visible inside. Chief Franklin's vehicle was parked two blocks farther down, on the opposite side of the road, but facing them. Nick signaled for a right turn, deciding that it would be too risky to pass that close to the chief.

As he went down the side street, he noticed a second car pulling up behind Chief Franklin's. If he hadn't turned, whoever that was would have seen them coming.

"Did you see who that was in the second car?" Drew asked.

"No, but it looks like a meeting or a weapons deal's going down. We'll have to go in on foot for a closer look."

Once out of sight of both cars, Nick killed their headlights and parked on the shoulder.

They climbed out, and as they came into view of the cars, they took cover. Working through the brush, they stopped almost even with the front of Franklin's car and peered out.

The driver of the car parked behind Franklin's climbed out and stood behind his open door for a moment, looking all around.

"That's Coyote," Nick said, seeing the man's face clearly, thanks to the dome light in the arms dealer's car.

Coyote's glance swept past their location, but if he saw them he didn't react. A moment later, he walked toward Franklin's car.

Franklin climbed out of the vehicle to meet him and the two men stood face to face, talking. Their voices were muted, too much so to be understood.

"Where's Koval?" Drew whispered. "Shouldn't he be around here somewhere?"

Hearing someone walking toward them through the brush and making no attempt to hide his arrival, Drew tilted her head toward the approaching figure, expecting to see Koval.

As Nick turned to look, the man raised a pistol and fired. There was a flash and Nick felt the tug on his sleeve from the near miss, but all he heard was the low thump of a silencer.

Nick grabbed Drew's hand, dropped down into an empty ditch, and raced into the bosque—the forested area that lined the river.

Nick led Drew into a thick grove of cottonwoods and stopped, pulling her to her knees and against him as he ducked. Over their own labored breathing, he heard people moving toward them from two different directions, and could see beams of flashlights flickering through the underbrush.

"We're outnumbered," he said. "We can't outrun them or hide here for long. We'll have to go after them individually. That's our only chance."

"What do we do?" Drew asked.

"I'm going to get the attention of the guy closest to us, the one with the silenced pistol, then lead him past you. As soon as he goes by, aim for his legs and Taser him," he said.

handing her the nonlethal device. "You've gone through our security workshops, right? Then just aim and shoot."

"In theory, I know what to do. But what if I miss, or the connectors don't make contact?" she asked, suddenly more afraid than ever.

"His slacks won't be as thick as his jacket, so there shouldn't be a problem. You won't miss. Crouch as low to the ground as you can and stay perfectly still until he goes by. You'll hear me first, then him. As he passes by you, I'll do something to make sure he looks in my direction."

As he slipped away, Drew stared at the yellow device in her hand. She'd held one once during an orientation, and knew how it operated, but she'd never actually fired one.

Hearing a noise to her right, Drew ducked down and listened.

The man trailing Nick taunted him softly. "Man up, Indian. If you show yourself now, I may let the woman live."

She'd been afraid before, but now she was just ticked off. If this idiot thought that she'd stand by while he shot Nick, he was about to get one huge reality check.

Nick hurried past her, snapping twigs and brush, deliberately being noisy so he could give away his position.

Drew remained totally still, then saw a shape emerge out of the dark, pistol in hand. As soon as he moved past her, Drew rose to full height and fired, hitting him in the back of his thigh. The man fell to the ground instantly, his body twitching.

Nick ran over and picked up the man's gun while Drew turned off the Taser. Working together, they quickly handcuffed their assailant's arms around a tree about three feet in diameter. Taking off one of the dazed suspect's shoes, Nick jammed the man's sock into his mouth so he couldn't yell out a warning.

Nick prepared the Taser for another shot, then handed it

back to her. "Keep this handy. We have at least two more bad guys to deal with."

"Do you know who this man is?"

"He's an ex-con named Johnson, another one of Coyote's associates."

As they stood, a twig snapped behind Drew. Nick pushed her to the ground, but before he could reach for his pistol, Coyote stepped out of the brush, his gun pointed at Nick's chest.

"Put your weapon on the ground, boy. Don't make this any more difficult on yourself," Coyote drawled, then waited as Nick did what he asked. "You're both going to die. The only choice you've got is whether the lady goes first or you do."

Nick stepped in front of Drew, knowing that was the only way he had left to protect her. He wouldn't be able to draw his backup pistol before Coyote fired.

Drew stepped out from behind Nick. "If this is where it ends for us, then we'll go side-by-side."

Nick watched the gunman's eyes. If Coyote hesitated, trying to decide who his first target would be, he'd have the opening he needed.

"Who gets it first?" Coyote asked in a bored voice, moving the barrel of the weapon from Nick to Drew. "Any last requests?"

Suddenly a shot rang out and a hole appeared in Coyote's chest right over his heart. Coyote looked surprised, but his expression soon faded as he slumped to the ground, blood oozing from the wound in his chest.

Nick dove to the ground and rolled, taking Drew with him. Weapon in hand, he was ready to fire when Chief Franklin stepped into full view.

Franklin's pistol was aimed at Nick's head from a distance of less than ten feet—a sure killshot.

"I can see you're wearing a vest, Blacksheep, so I'll have to make it a head shot, I guess."

"Lower your weapon, Chief, before it's too late. I may go down, but you'll be dead right along with me."

Franklin looked at both their faces, his weapon never wavering. "I can't put my weapon down. It's gone too far for that. But if you shoot, I shoot, and we both lose. So let's negotiate instead. I've got a real win-win solution for you. I've got more cash than I'll ever use, and I'm about to retire. So how about this? You get the credit for bagging Coyote and Johnson, and I reward you with, say, a hundred thousand in untraceable bills. We both walk away wealthy. You'll be a live hero, and we'll all get to finish our lives in relative comfort."

Nick rose to his feet, his gun still pointed at Franklin's chest.

Drew also stood slowly, reaching into her pocket as she did and putting her hand on the Taser. "Listen to him, Nick. That's a lot of money. We could make a brand new future for ourselves," she said, stepping away from Nick ever so slightly. If she could widen the gap between them, then Chief Franklin would have two distinct targets. With his attention divided, she'd be able to draw the Taser and fire. But it wasn't a quick-draw weapon. What if it snagged on her pocket? She pushed back her uncertainty.

Franklin kept his focus on the person he considered his greatest threat, Nick. "Listen to me, son. I spent all of my life working for the citizens of this town. And what thanks did I get? A pension that'll barely make my house payment. A man gets few chances to break out of the middle ground, and I took mine. Do you have what it takes, or do we die out here for nothing?" He paused. "And just so we're clear. Your lady will go, too."

"Not where you're going," Drew said, yanking the Taser from her pocket and firing.

As the contacts hit, Franklin's body twitched and his hands jerked uncontrollably. His gun went off, but the bullet went wild. Franklin hit the ground, his body contorted, his muscles seizing up.

Their enemy incapacitated, Drew flicked the power off. While Nick worked to securely tie up the chief with his own belt, Drew called for backup.

"We'll have help shortly," she told Nick, a moment later.

"We need to find Koval. Harry could be wounded—or worse."

"Nah," a familiar voice coming through the brush said. "I took a hit, but the vest kept me in one piece." Koval stumbled over to them, rubbing his chest. "I left the cruiser for a closer look and Coyote's man caught me off guard. He shot me at close range twice. The hits incapacitated me for a bit, but the vest held."

Koval glanced down at the chief. "Wanna borrow my cuffs?" The detective removed a set of handcuffs from his belt, groaning from the effort, and tossed them on the ground beside Nick. "Looks like I missed all the fun."

"*Fun?* Men!" Drew snapped, and threw her hands up in the air. "You're all nuts!"

Koval looked at Nick and shrugged. "Women. So emotional. How'd you end up with her anyway?"

"Luck of the draw," Nick answered.

Drew glared at Koval and then back at Nick, but before she could say anything else, sirens filled the air.

TRAVIS STOOD NEXT TO NICK as the chief was loaded into the rear seat of a cruiser. "Not a bad job, bro," Travis said. "Johnson's already offering a deal, volunteering to rat out Slick for the shootings, and Franklin for dealing with Coyote. But that's just frosting on the cake. The AK was still in the chief's trunk, and his prints will be all over the weapon and the case he used to carry it from the station. The local FBI and ATF have warrants to search for more weapons inside his house, too. The crime scene team is heading there next, and I'm going over to help them out. Do you need anything from me before I leave?"

Nick's gaze stayed on Drew, who was seated on the step of the crime-scene van, giving her statement to Captain Wright and Detective Koval. "When I thought I was about to die, I found that I only had one regret," Nick said, slowly. "I've spent too much time thinking about the past. That's not living—that's wasting life."

"And now you're ready to look ahead?" Travis followed Nick's line of sight and watched Drew for a moment. "You've got a winner there, bro. She'll drive you crazy, but you'll never get bored."

"What I have to do now is put the past behind me for good. It's time for me to have a Sing done."

"I know the right *hataalii* for this," he said, writing down a name, phone number, and drawing a quick map. "He can probably do a ceremony right away for you at Long Mountain, if you make the call now. Once summer arrives, you can return and have a full ceremony done, with all our family present and your new wife."

"Wife..." Nick smiled. "That's not a done deal, not yet, anyway."

By the time he finished making the call, Drew was ready to go. Nick walked her back to the pickup, and away from prying eyes gathered her into his arms. As he held her tightly against him, he struggled to find the right words to tell her how much she meant to him.

Instead of the flowery language he knew women loved, all he could come up with was, "You did good out here today."

"You're just saying that because I didn't argue with you."

"Don't ruin it." Bending down, he took her mouth in a long, tender kiss, filled with all the emotions he hadn't been able to put into words.

When he drew back at long last, he heard her sigh. "I've made arrangements to see a medicine man—what we call a *hataalii*," he said. "It's time to go to Long Mountain. Will you come with me? Afterwards…there are things I need to say to you."

"Where's Long Mountain?" she asked. "Not that it matters," she added, before he could answer. "I'll be ready to go whenever you are."

"We have to leave right away. Part of the ritual has to be concluded before dawn, and there are preparations to be made."

"Lead—I'll follow—for now," she added, with a hint of a smile.

He laughed. "Is it always going to be this way?"

She smiled. "You already know the answer."

Epilogue

They arrived well past midnight. Long Mountain wasn't really a mountain—it was a large rock formation west of Kayenta, on the Arizona portion of the Navajo Nation. As they arrived at the site, the *hataalii,* wearing the traditional blue sash of a medicine man around his forehead, greeted them. A much older Navajo man, his assistant, stood behind him. Both were wrapped in blankets to ward off the winter cold.

"We can begin whenever you're ready," the *hataalii* said.

Drew took a seat to the north of the fire, while Nick sat on the medicine man's left. The other Navajo man maintained the fire.

The *hataalii* studied the moon and stars above them, positioned himself, then began a monotone chant. At certain points, he pressed bundles of herbs against Nick's body. Then, at long last, he untied the thread that bound all the bundles together.

"This will free him," the *hataalii* whispered, as he went past Drew, then continued chanting.

Although Drew didn't fully understand the ritual, she could feel its power. Something assured her that after it was over, neither Nick nor she would ever be the same again.

The medicine man applied a salve to Nick's face and then placed some on Drew's. "This blackening will frighten evil and make it fear you," the *hataalii* said, helping her understand.

THE RITUAL CONTINUED WITHOUT interruption until first light. As the sun peered over the eastern horizon, the *hataalii* nodded. "Now it is beautiful again."

Bowing his head in respect, Nick answered. "Thank you."

The medicine man handed Nick a token of the ceremony— an eagle feather. "You've now been freed. This token symbolizes the indestructibility of your spirit. Take it and go in beauty."

After the *hataalii* and his assistant drove away, Drew and Nick stood side-by-side. In the first rays of dawn, with the streaks of blackening on his face, Nick looked primitive and wild, and a master of his element.

Nick took the ceremonial token he'd received and pressed it into her hand, wrapping her fingers around it. "The Navajo Way teaches that whatever happens to this ceremonial token will also happen to me. I now give it to you, the woman who taught me about love, along with my heart. Will you walk the trail of beauty with me today and for as many tomorrows as we're given?"

"Yes," she whispered as his lips closed over hers.

COMING NEXT MONTH

Available September 14, 2010

#2035 WHAT A WESTMORELAND WANTS
Brenda Jackson
Man of the Month

#2036 EXPECTING THE RANCHER'S HEIR
Kathie DeNosky
Dynasties: The Jarrods

#2037 DANTE'S TEMPORARY FIANCÉE
Day Leclaire
The Dante Legacy

#2038 STAND-IN BRIDE'S SEDUCTION
Yvonne Lindsay
Wed at any Price

#2039 AT THE BILLIONAIRE'S BECK AND CALL?
Rachel Bailey

#2040 THE SECRET CHILD & THE COWBOY CEO
Janice Maynard

SDCNM0810

LARGER-PRINT BOOKS!

GET 2 FREE LARGER-PRINT NOVELS
PLUS 2 FREE GIFTS!

❖ HARLEQUIN®

INTRIGUE®

Breathtaking Romantic Suspense

YES! Please send me 2 FREE LARGER-PRINT Harlequin Intrigue® novels and my 2 FREE gifts (gifts are worth about $10). After receiving them, if I don't wish to receive any more books, I can return the shipping statement marked "cancel." If I don't cancel, I will receive 6 brand-new novels every month and be billed just $4.99 per book in the U.S. or $5.74 per book in Canada. That's a saving of at least 13% off the cover price! It's quite a bargain! Shipping and handling is just 50¢ per book.* I understand that accepting the 2 free books and gifts places me under no obligation to buy anything. I can always return a shipment and cancel at any time. Even if I never buy another book from Harlequin, the two free books and gifts are mine to keep forever.

199/399 HDN E5MS

Name   (PLEASE PRINT)

Address   Apt. #

City   State/Prov.   Zip/Postal Code

Signature (if under 18, a parent or guardian must sign)

Mail to the **Harlequin Reader Service:**
IN U.S.A.: P.O. Box 1867, Buffalo, NY 14240-1867
IN CANADA: P.O. Box 609, Fort Erie, Ontario L2A 5X3
Not valid for current subscribers to Harlequin Intrigue Larger-Print books.

**Are you a subscriber to Harlequin Intrigue books and
want to receive the larger-print edition? Call 1-800-873-8635 today!**

* Terms and prices subject to change without notice. Prices do not include applicable taxes. N.Y. residents add applicable sales tax. Canadian residents will be charged applicable provincial taxes and GST. Offer not valid in Quebec. This offer is limited to one order per household. All orders subject to approval. Credit or debit balances in a customer's account(s) may be offset by any other outstanding balance owed by or to the customer. Please allow 4 to 6 weeks for delivery. Offer available while quantities last.

Your Privacy: Harlequin Books is committed to protecting your privacy. Our Privacy Policy is available online at www.eHarlequin.com or upon request from the Reader Service. From time to time we make our lists of customers available to reputable third parties who may have a product or service of interest to you. If you would prefer we not share your name and address, please check here. ☐

Help us get it right—We strive for accurate, respectful and relevant communications. To clarify or modify your communication preferences, visit us at www.ReaderService.com/consumerschoice.

HARLEQUIN®

A Romance

FOR EVERY MOOD™

Spotlight on
Heart & Home

Heartwarming romances
where love can happen
right when you least expect it.

See the next page to enjoy a sneak peek
from Harlequin Superromance®,
a Heart and Home series.

CATHHHSR10

*Enjoy a sneak peek at fan favorite Molly O'Keefe's
Harlequin Superromance miniseries,*
THE NOTORIOUS O'NEILLS, *with*
TYLER O'NEILL'S REDEMPTION,
*available September 2010
only from Harlequin Superromance.*

Police chief Juliette Tremblant recognized the shape of the man strolling down the street—in as calm and leisurely fashion as if it were the middle of the day rather than midnight. She slowed her car, convinced her eyes were playing tricks on her. It had been a long time since Tyler O'Neill had been seen in this town.

As she pulled to a stop at the curb, he turned toward her, and her heart about stopped.

"What the hell are you doing here, Tyler?"

"Well, if it isn't Juliette Tremblant." He made his way over to her, then leaned down so he could look her in the eye. He was close enough to touch.

Juliette was not, repeat, *not* going to touch Tyler O'Neill. Not with her fingers. Not with a ten-foot pole. There would be no touching. Which was too bad, since it was the only way she was ever going to convince herself the man standing in front of her—as rumpled and heart-stoppingly handsome now as he'd been at sixteen—was real.

And not a figment of all her furious revenge dreams.

"What are you doing back in Bonne Terre?" she asked.

"The manor is sitting empty," Tyler said and shrugged, as though his arriving out of the blue after ten years was casual. "Seems like someone should be watching over the family home."

"You?" She laughed at the very notion of him being here for any unselfish reason. "Please."

HSREXP0910

He stared at her for a second, then smiled. Her heart fluttered against her chest—a small mechanical bird powered by that smile.

"You're right." But that cryptic comment was all he offered.

Juliette bit her lip against the other questions.

Why did you go?

Why didn't you write? Call?

What did I do?

But what would be the point? Ten years of silence were all the answer she really needed.

She had sworn off feeling anything for this man long ago. Yet one look at him and all the old hurt and rage resurfaced as though they'd been waiting for the chance. That made her mad.

She put the car in gear, determined not to waste another minute thinking about Tyler O'Neill. "Have a good night, Tyler," she said, liking all the cool "go screw yourself" she managed to fit into those words.

It seems Juliette has an old score to settle with Tyler.
Pick up TYLER O'NEILL'S REDEMPTION
to see how he makes it up to her.
Available September 2010,
only from Harlequin Superromance.

Copyright © 2010 by Molly Fader

HSREXP0910

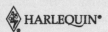

HARLEQUIN®

INTRIGUE®

Five brothers, one mystery

JOANNA WAYNE

brings an all-new suspenseful series of five
brothers searching for the truth behind their
mother's murder and their father's unknown past.

Will their journey allow them
to uncover the truth and open their hearts?

Find out in the first installment:

COWBOY SWAGGER

Available September 2010

Look for more
SONS OF TROY LEDGER
stories coming soon!

www.eHarlequin.com

HI69495